the sonnets

the sonnets

A Novel

LENNARD J. DAVIS

STATE UNIVERSITY OF NEW YORK PRESS

Cover Illustration of "The Dude" by Kevin Chadwick, Chadwick Design Inc.

Published by
State University of New York Press, Albany

For information, address State University of New York Press,
90 State Street, Suite 700, Albany, N.Y., 12207

Production by Kelli Williams
Marketing by Michael Campochiaro

Library of Congress Cataloging-in-Publication Data
Davis, Lennard J., 1949–
    The sonnets : a novel / Lennard J. Davis.
        p. cm.
    ISBN 0-7914-4977-7 (acid free)—ISBN 0-7914-4978-5 (pbk. : acid free)
    1. English teachers—Fiction. 2. Manhattan (New York, N.Y.)—Fiction. I. Title.

PS3554.A935 S66 2001
813'.54—dc21   00-061229

10 9 8 7 6 5 4 3 2 1

contents

1

THE ONLY BEGETTER

Illness is a kind of cure. The worse the better. Or illness is a kind of journey promising all happiness, wishing the well-wishing adventurer eternity in his setting forth. I am writing in the fever of a sickness, a malaise that wants recovery. I have before me the image of a face the cause and cure of all. It is a beautiful face, a fair face that now begins to form another. How could so fair a face ravage mine to this degree?

My story begins on a misty afternoon in Manhattan. I was looking out from the window of my study at the scudding vapors that appeared and disappeared over the dark waters of the Hudson River. I was in that half-focused state of distraction, in the midst of writing when writing has ceased, when there is desire without object. My children were playing in a living room accompanied by the indistinct gabbling of the television. On the screen, in the distance, some show about small round creatures whose cuteness is a pleasure to children and a torment to everyone else.

By now the sun was setting over Riverside Park, the sky igniting into the mauve and orange that is the gift of pollution refracted by crepuscular light. I thought the sun looked like a rose that would never die. My wife walked in and said, "There's someone at the door for you."

"Do I know him?"

"*I* don't know him."

It was unusual to have a visit from someone I did not know. My life was a compact, well-joined scheme. I was forty and married. Two kids. A girl eight and a boy eleven. A professor of literature at Columbia University. My specialty—Shakespeare. My life up till this point will not much interest anyone. That is why I have to detail it. Each day I rise at 7:30, the alarm clock set to WQXR so that classical music might nudge me out of my strange, dark sleep and make my day possible. I go into my daughter's room and kiss the softly entranced cheek as if I were her morning prince, watch her eyes open, see her chew her lip and close her eyes again. And there is the temptation to let her sleep, let everything sleep, let time drift without form or structure.

But I wake her, giving form to her vision, and when she knows enough, she smiles and puts her arm around my neck. I lift her up and carry her to the bathroom. If I look quickly, I can accept what the night has done to my face. I see the trenches dug into my forehead and the deep sunken eyes looking back at me. I don't look for long, but turn my gaze to my daughter's smooth, blushed cheek. Then I wake my son. Since he is older, he grunts and turns over wishing me gone, some might say "dead." The children and I have breakfast, my wife having gone to work. I walk with the kids along Riverside Drive to their school. We notice the change of seasons and the patterns birds in flight make over the graded waters of the Hudson. I watch the children as they surge into their haze of friends. I watch my connection with their childhood severed. Then I go to my office.

There I spend my day. I teach my classes, see students, engage in the general intrigues of academic life that are made strange and vicious because what is at stake is merely the imago of reputation and honor rather than the cold clink of money. Then I come home. I have a drink, make supper, and work on my book at night. My wife and I read in bed. The children go to sleep, and then after a while so do we. Twice a week we make love.

I am not implying mine is a boring life. My wife and I go to the theater, to galleries, we walk on the street and observe the human pageant. I clip restaurant reviews from the *New York Times* and then on special occasions venture into the stark or ornate opulence of rooms where we bask in the particular pleasures food brings. We entertain friends. We have a second home on Martha's Vineyard where we spend productive vacations and the entire languorous summer.

So when someone shows up at my door whom I do not know, I would most likely be surprised. I know everyone who is likely to call on me.

When I saw him the first thing I thought was how handsome he was, almost like a girl. I thought of the lines from the *Sonnets*:

> Thou art thy mothers glasse and she in thee
> Calls backe the lovely Aprill of her prime . . .

That was an unlikely thought for me because I do not usually regard men as handsome. I am not disposed that way.

Standing before me was a someone in his twenties with long, straight, blonde hair, a prominent forehead, intense eyes and full lips. He was wearing denims and a leather jacket that was smooth and burnished by use. He smiled at me.

"Professor Marlow, you probably don't remember me. I was your student." He paused. "Christopher Johnson? I was in your Shakespeare course a few years ago? Well, actually I audited it." Everything he said ended in a rising inflection, characteristic of his generation, as if the words were flying up and gathering on the ceiling.

"I don't remember . . . exactly."

"I wrote the paper [the words went up] on the idea of sexual death in Shakespeare's poetry [up again]."

"Yes . . . " I really had no idea.

"I'm sorry to bother you, especially at home, but I was won-dering if you could answer a question?"

"Yes . . . " Said the way one does when trying to be civil while not being civil at all. I don't encourage students to visit me at home. In fact, I loathe the idea.

I was about to tell him to leave when I noticed a drop of blood, almost imperceptible, fall from his hand onto the floor. He looked down and then up at me. Another drop fell, and he tried to cover the spot by stepping on it, but the gesture was futile, although polite. The drops smeared against the oak floor.

"I'm sorry . . . I . . . "

"That's all right. Are you . . . ?"

"I'm fine. It's nothing." He took out a tissue and bent over to clean up the drops, but more, like tiny gems, slid down his arm and fell onto the floor. He trembled a bit as if he were cold, as if the blood carried some undetermined warmth out of his body.

My wife walked in and looked alarmed.

"This is a former student of mine, Anne."

She looked at the blood.

"He seems to have cut himself on the elevator up here. Could you get him something?"

"Of course."

She returned in minutes with a few Band-Aids and some antiseptic.

While she was gone, the young man looked at me with a gaze that seemed, I am discomposed to say it, lovely. It had a sadness I can only remember but cannot describe. It was like a sadness of the lover who must separate from his beloved and go on a long and dangerous journey—the look that men gave their women when they went off to Normandy, to Korea, to Vietnam. There was both helplessness and confidence in the look; some hope and not a little despair.

The sound of the television seeped into the room at our feet and then rose to the ceiling to join the spent words of the young man. Through the window, the mists were mingling with the pollution as the last light of day was shot through with a greenish yellow, the *rayon vert* we so rarely get to see at the moment of sunset. It was winter, a hideous one I might add. The difficulty was not so much with the snow, but with the constant fluctuation between snow and rain, so that everything tended to freeze and unfreeze each day. The following day was a new thaw, and the succeeding night a new freeze. Old women were breaking their hips and femurs at record pace. The sap kept rising in the trees and then being checked with frost. I wanted spring, and could only look at preserved flowers and smell the essential oils pent up in bottles on Anne's bureau. That was the only sweetness in this hard winter.

I took the Band-Aids from Anne and asked the young man to sit down.

"Roll up your sleeve, Chris, and let's have a look." I said avuncularly.

He obeyed, and as he rolled up his sleeve I saw that his arm was lined with scars very neatly arranged in parallel rows. There was something shocking about this scarification, and something beautiful as well. I thought of the dessert *mille feuilles*—a thousand leaves—that pastry made by folding dough with butter over and over again until there were a thousand folds of the thinnest dough. All the scars were healed except for the most recent one, a small red line cut deep into the flesh. It made a boundary between the scarred part of his very white flesh and the unscarred part. There must have been closer to a hundred scars than a thousand. The cut itself had laid bare the outer skin and revealed the red, dark interior of the inside of his arm with a surgical precision. I stared at this defacement with a kind of fascination, looking into him and wondering what had made him commit this obvious self-mutilation.

The next thing I thought about was AIDS. This is how we think—blood and AIDS, sex and AIDS. I felt callow about the connection. But I took the antiseptic and applied it to the cut, anyway. He winced a bit, although I used Betadine, which does not sting. The Band-Aids were obviously inadequate, so I looked into the hamper. All I could find was my son's underpants. I was aware of the bad metonymy, but nevertheless I ripped the cloth and tied it around his arm. Within seconds the underpants began to blossom into red, first faintly then with more vermillion, and finally became so red that I had to change the dressing within minutes.

I did not want to pry, but I said. "What is this?"

"I cut myself."

"I can see that . . . "

"No, I mean I cut myself. That is what I do. I use a razor blade."

I looked blank, not wanting to show any emotion that might condescend to his confession.

"I can't really help it."

I nodded. What could I say?

I heard my wife coming back, and, not certain why, I pulled his sleeve over his arm. Perhaps I was being protective. Of whom, I'm not sure, though. I didn't want to disturb her, but I also didn't want her to know what I had seen. There was a faint moment of betrayal in the act, in the way an unfaithful husband covers a love letter with his sleeve, a gesture made casual by an instant of deliberation.

"What was your question? You said you came because you had a question for me?" I asked changing the subject.

"Well, I was having a discussion with a friend, and we were wondering about tragi-comedy. Like why it is that Shakespeare mixed tragedy with comedy. I mean that isn't a logical thing . . . "

Anne walked in with some wine.

"Everything okay now?"

"Fine," I said. And Christopher smiled as if nothing had happened. This was just between men.

She looked quizzically at me and said.

"Well, dinner's almost ready . . ."

"Are you staying . . . ?" I asked the young man reflexively before I even thought about the wisdom of doing so.

"If . . . "

"No, it's fine." It was too late to withdraw the offer.

"Well, I don't want to ..."

"No, really, it's fine."

"Then, yes, if it's really..."

"Yes, don't worry. It's fine."

Anne left the room, and Christopher quickly said in a low voice.

"When you write about this ... if you do ... but I'm sure, well, almost sure you will, you know, don't make it ... um ... sordid. It could be ..." He searched for the words. "... sort of ..."

"When I ... but I don't write those kind of books."

"I know what you write. I've read it all. I read *Bodies of Knowledge* and *Tortured Sleep* and what was the other? Oh. *Bard's Desire.*"

One could not help feel flattered. We professors are venal. We spend our days in front of a class of students trying to elicit admiration, respect, and, well, love, and then we spend our nights writing books that we hope will elicit admiration, respect, and, well, love. The irony is that no one reads our works besides other academics. Our readers are the very people primed to attack us so they might clear the field for their own book which they wish will be the one to elicit admiration and desire. Consequently, we're easily flattered by anyone who reads, or claims to have read, what we write.

"I'm working on a new book," I found myself a bit shame-facedly confessing. "It's just called *The Sonnets* but it has a rather remarkable thesis ..."

He was tying another strip around his arm, throwing the bloodstained one into my wastebasket. I looked into the basket, which is really only designed for paper, and saw the carmine stain seep by capillary action into the cardboard walls. I thought about AIDS again and resolved to throw the wastebasket out tonight before the children could touch it.

"Well, I've got a new ..."

I was going to continue, but we were called for dinner.

2

DENY THAT THOU BEAR'ST LOVE TO ANY

Spaghetti and tofu meatballs. Did I mention that we were vegetarians? Christopher looked a bit disconcerted.

"It's tofu meatballs," I explained apologetically.

The kids were beginning to make playful designs out of their food.

"That's fine," he said.

"We're vegetarians."

"I'm not. I do eat meat but only something I'd feel comfortable killing. I wouldn't kill a cow, but I could kill a chicken."

The kids looked a little shocked, something about the familiarity of chickens in their story books. The sky was falling.

"I've killed chickens on the farm. I grew up in Nebraska, and we had chickens. It was my job. Well, actually I liked wringing their necks."

A gloomy silence spread around the table. I looked at the clock and saw that the day was sunk into night. Anne looked a little aghast. I suddenly felt old and prissy at the same time.

"What's awful is the sound of the neck. It just goes snap, really a crack. You can feel the life drain out of it. It's exciting."

"Dear," Anne said, "don't we know someone from Nebraska?" She turned to Christopher, hoping to change the subject. My son was making dying chicken sounds. "Where are you from?"

"Lincoln. But I'm really from San Diego. My parents moved out to Nebraska when I was six."

"Oh, and what are you doing in New York?"

"Trying to make it as an actor, meaning that during the day I'm waiting tables."

"Where are you living?" I asked.

"In the Village. I'm staying with my girlfriend. We've been together since college. In fact, she was in your class with me—Sarah Molkowitz?"

The faces of countless young women flashed before me. They all had long black hair, olive complexions, and somewhat Jewish faces. They were intelligent, and they were dressed in a range of clothes from hip huggers to Lycra mini-skirts, from flowered blouses to flannel shirts and baby tees, from black gothic to spiked punk. They spanned my twenty years of teaching, filling the space with their earnest eyes, questioning glances, and diligent note taking. I called out to all of them sitting in the seminar room of my mind. None of them seemed to respond to the name of Sarah Molkowitz. I shook my head. I didn't know her. I barely knew him.

What was there about him, this boy from the American heartlands who had wrung the necks of chickens? The sensuousness of his lips, or the matter-of-fact way he spoke to us? He was a stretch of Interstate 80 sitting at my New York table.

"So that sounds serious," said Anne beginning to tread a little heavily. I tend to think of myself as urban and therefore urbane, but she was from the suburbs, New Canaan, Connecticut, and always managed to say something that disconcerted me a bit. Anne learned her social graces at boarding school, and there were still grating moments of behavior that came from rich girls rubbing their granite hackles against each other.

"I don't really think much of marriage. It's just a bourgeois institution. This romantic ideology, it's deployed all over to keep everyone in check." Too many courses in cultural studies had addled his vocabulary. He could talk the talk, but did he walk the walk?

"That's all right," I said, "I agree. Anne and I lived together for a long time. We only decided to get married because it was too complicated to have kids, draw up a contract."

"I hate children, too."

Another pause.

I looked carefully at his face, and I felt a ridiculous feeling of attraction. How can I say this? He looked like a girl to me. Not exactly a girl, but like a girl. What happens to men as they get older? To them, youth begins to look like beauty, however it is gendered. I wondered how he would look at my age. I could see, overlaid on his young face, the creases in his brow, the marks at the corner of the eyes, the sunken puffy sickliness under the eyes, the expanding belly. It was as if my vision had become one of those magic writing tablets we used as children. When the cover was lifted, the lines disappeared. I didn't like the way the wrinkles looked against his young face, so I pulled up the cellophane sheet, and he was back to his youthful regard. I wished I could do the same for myself.

About this attraction. I tried to ignore it, but that didn't work.

"Children aren't so bad," I found myself saying. My son and daughter looked at me as though I were considering putting them out with the evening's garbage.

"No offense . . . " Christopher added apologetically.

"None taken. But they are the future. We live through them. They are little perfect copies of us." I could not have come up with more cliches if I tried. I had become the breeder chamber of commerce for bourgeois marriage, reproduction, and respectability. "They are our immortality."

"And yet they die, too, don't they?"

This thought percolated instantly through my children, who at that moment seemed to receive the fatal kiss of mortality on their still immortal skin. I could see the shadow of death pass over them, and I could hear the creak of its lugubrious wings. I looked at the clock. It was getting late. I looked out the window. It had begun to rain.

"Yes, they die. But then there is something in the fact that they have children, too."

"And so on, ad infinitum . . ." he said.

I had nothing to add, so I said, "It's a hideous night." We could hear the Riverside Drive wind, famously treacherous along the Upper West Side for its knife-like precision in cutting through outer garments, whisk through the lofty, barren trees. "You know, like that Ogden Nash poem

> Big fish have little fish
> on their backs to bite 'em
> and so on *ad infinitum*."

He laughed and tightened his makeshift bandage. No one else laughed. It was getting late. The children were cranky and began to fight, as if to prove his point about how loathsome children are.

"I'm sorry," he said. "I'm not myself tonight, which is strange because you don't know me, anyway." If he was not himself tonight, then who was I finding so dangerously interesting?

"Normally, I'm more upbeat." When he said the word "upbeat" his lips moved in slow motion. I found myself thinking of kissing them, they seemed like sweet forms, sweet semblances. I stopped myself, feeling foolish, wondering what a man my age did with these feelings? I was like a father to his son.

How does it happen that a lifelong heterosexual man finds another man attractive? Maybe it happens by degrees. There is sometimes a mistake. You see what you think is young woman, and you look twice, give a stare of attraction across the great anonymous void of the street, but then it turns out you are wrong. The young woman is a young man. Once, years ago, when I was a student, I was walking in *Le Cascine* in Florence and saw, really stared at, some slinky prostitutes. Cars were driving by with men in them. Some of the prostitutes got in, others got out. These were young, slim, beautiful women . . . only they were men. It took me weeks to realize it. I had to admire them, even if they were men. Or because they were men. I almost took one back to my hotel. She looked like the sexiest thing I ever envisioned, but when I approached with money in my trembling hand, I could see the hair follicles embedded in her skin as indelible reminders of masculinity, and, despite the deep vermillion of her lips, I could not go through with it. I asked her for the time.

Maybe experiences like these prepare you for this moment. It happens when you read *Death in Venice*, and the mysterious hypnosis of the novel lets Tadeus pass Eschenbach's eyes, which are really your eyes. You admire him because you are a captive of the novel, of the novelist. This could happen to you, even now. Or in *The Crying Game* when you find out that the object of your desire is a man, and the film makes you not care about it. Or when you see the shine of young hair on the head of a young man. Or if you admire a single feature—clear skin, blue eyes, dreadlocks. You begin, like Plato's lover, to admire the feature and the mark of beauty, and you become tired, world weary, of anchoring it to a gender. You simply admire beauty, life, energy. Everything that grows is only perfect for a moment. And then you think it would be right to kiss that moment. To kiss beauty, energy, life because at the very moment time debates with decay.

I said good night to Christopher at the door. He seemed familiar to me now, and I wanted to put my arms around him as I would a friend. What flooded through me was the cool reserve of my age, my position, what is expected of me. What ebbed back again was warmth, rebellion, and the desire to do what one wants that comes with impatience of being a certain age.

"Your question," I said, "I didn't answer it."

"That's all right. There's plenty of time."

"But the idea of tragi-comedy, it's really more about two worlds meeting in a moment between fear and laughter. The kind of fear that breaks the body down, throws it off a building. And laughter that makes life ridiculous. That saves it. The tragic makes the comedy bleed, and the comedy sets the tragedy on fire."

"And the comic makes the tragic funny?"

"No, not funny. More tragic."

"I don't get it."

"Well, there's plenty of time to explain."

I shook his hand, and we said good night. I wanted to graft something new into the hackneyed salutation.

"Bye," I said. But somewhere, in a parallel universe, I put my arms around his broad shoulders and kissed him. As a father kisses a son. Only that, I told myself. Then I closed the door, which uttered a low, booming click as the lock caught.

3

IF I COULD WRITE THE BEAUTY OF YOUR EYES

Days passed. It doesn't matter how many, but if we give it a number, let it be sixteen. I was never much of a cabalist. I was in my office when the phone rang. I hadn't been obsessing about Christopher. In fact, I had all but forgotten him as one all but forgets a pleasant thought. The bottom of my wastebasket was still stained with blood. The blood had turned dark brown, nothing more than a stain. I thought, why throw it away? The AIDS virus dies quickly on exposure to air. That's what they said. So I kept it.

The phone rang. It was Norman Goldman. He was "our Poet." Every university English department has one. And despite small differences, they're all the same. They tend to be big men in their fifties or early sixties. They wear beards and bring their German Shepherds to school. Their offices are unkempt, piled high with old issues of *Sewanee Review* and *Antaeus*, one of which a bit too long ago printed their cycle of poems about sex and mountains and Zen. This is the office where frail, blonde women who smell of Gauloise cigarettes mixed with attar of roses or patchouli oil come in and sit on part of a large dark chair, while they look up into The Poet's face and ponder eternity, thinking, "Do I dare?"

Goldman was such a man. He was the New Zealand varia-tion, which gave him a patina of Britishness and a touch of rugged pioneer. This combination made him even more adored in this Anglophilic hot house of a university, which doesn't bother to distinguish accents of the British Empire as long as there is some hint of culture and foreignness.

He was a poet before he was anything else. His attitude toward the rest of us, who only analyzed literature and variously thought of it as cultural repression, or transgression, or clitoral play, was that subtle but unmistakable form of condescension reserved for those incapable of learning the swerve and heft of language beyond its mere utility. Toward me, no theorist but simply a dogged reader with a historical interest in things, he felt a bit warmer, such as one might feel toward an accountant who had done a good job of preparing the tax returns.

I first met Norman when he was poet-in-residence in Auckland University. I was traveling around New Zealand on a Fulbright lecturing about the history of hunchbacks and Shakespeare's use of deformity in *Richard III*. There is a very good book to be written on this subject, but because of time commitments I will not be the person to do it. New Zealand was a disappointment for me. I had read that it was the most remote place in the world—the farthest from any other land mass. It was the place most recently colonized by humans. So I expected nature in its undergarments; the Maori as inhabitants of an Edenic world. What I found somewhat resembled parts of New Jersey in Bermuda shorts. The entire North Island looked like it had been built for impoverished people in the 1950s. Every street in every town resembled Paramus or Wildwood, New Jersey. Having been thus disillusioned, I then met Norman and was further repelled.

Norman was a swollen, overweight man in his fifties. His hair was slapped down on his poetic pate with several years' worth of oleaginous grime. His large stomach protruded through his poly-cotton shirts, and he wore a beat-up Australian bush hat at all times. His large German Shepherd named Nagg followed him wherever he went and smelled like a recipe for *eau de mange*. Despite this inventory of unappealing qualities, Norman trailed one of the most beautiful women I had ever seen. A tall, stately, Maori with a cultured New Zealand accent devoid of all the garish vowels, Delilah Te Kanowa had a body honed to perfection by vigorous exercise gained tramping in the bush every weekend. She was his muse, but you wondered immediately what was in it for her.

Norman was supposed to be my host in Auckland. He was the kind of host who telephoned you in your bungalow of a motel to suggest that you take him out to dinner. I had been traveling for several days, barely avoiding crashing my rental car as I drove on the wrong side of the road. I was looking for rest and a refined meal. We met in the best restaurant in Auckland— suspended over the harbor—ate huge quantities of raw oysters that tasted like the crystalline spume of the frigid Pacific, and quaffed delicately oak-infused Chardonnays. When the bill came Norman looked over at Delilah and then at me. He said, "Awfully nice of you to pay for this. We New Zealanders don't get much of a salary compared to you Yanks."

Delilah smiled in gratitude as I erased the bill's debt with a swipe of my credit card. Somewhere in New York City, my bank account groaned as it was relieved of its meager contents, but I was plied with enough local wine to forget for whom the debt tolled. Then Norman managed to get me to pay for a nightclub tour and several bottles of vodka I bought for subsequent consumption but which I realized later I never saw again.

But that was only the beginning. When I returned to the States, I began getting e-mail from Norman saying that he was on his way from New Zealand to New York. He wanted to stay at our place in the city for a few days—and could Delilah and Nagg come too? I e-mailed back that we were pretty cramped for space and that I was busy writing my book. With a quick hit of the reply function he answered "So it's settled. I'll see you with great joy on Monday."

And he did. His great joy—not mine.

Norman showing up at one's door was like having the circus coming to stay. Not only did we get Norman, we got Nagg, his globe-trotting fleas, and puppies, since Nagg turned out to be a bitch. As did Delilah. The pleasure of seeing her perfect body lying on my furniture was greatly offset by her amazing slovenliness. Every article of clothing and every one of her possessions were on display in our living room where she took up residence. Needless to say, their two-day stay turned out to be a much longer one. Norman became poet-in-residence at our house. I have trouble remembering if it was weeks or months, but by the end of what seemed like years I put my foot down. This meant pushing through several geological layers of Delilah's underwear and gym apparel since now she had traded tramping in the bush for Stairmaster in the Columbia gym, borrowing Anne's ID whenever she needed to go.

I have had annoying guests, and each annoying guest has his or her own unique way of infuriating a host. But Norman had taken out a patent on the full panoply of annoying ways. His and Delilah's most annoying trait was a kind of pet parade of human sexuality. Norman announced he was "into" Eros—male or female it did not matter. He did more than announce, he sent out press releases. They made love on our couch at all hours of the day. Our children often would come running from the living room with simple questions about what appeared to be complex bodily configurations. Odd implements made of latex and leather would end up in the bathroom sink. I myself learned a thing or two by stumbling on bizarre contraptions left in the refrigerator next to the always dwindling food supplies. Loud groans and poignant sighs, yelps and savage whispers seemed to be on a tape loop that came out of the living room. The couch began to sag and the velvet became discolored with suggestive stains. Sometimes there were other people there, people we did not know, people that our local New Zealand chapter of Swinging Singles had met in some bar. I would see Norman come lumbering down the long hallway dripping in sweat that cascaded down his protuberant belly. He would give me a wink and open his eyes wide in mock amazement as he would whisper, "She's amazing!" Or Delilah would slip from the bathroom totally naked with a purple welt lazily rising from her back and trailing down her granite buttocks. Anne and I would tactfully mention that the children were perhaps being exposed to something they should not see.

"Nonsense," Norman would say nasally, "children know a lot more than you think. They have a deep, inborn evil uncorrupted by civilization. Why should they sit in their rooms and speculate? Reality never hurt anyone." "Adam and Eve. Blake. Walt Whitman," he would mutter telegraphically as he walked in a swaying, wobbling saunter down the hallway.

I finally got him out of my house by arranging to have the place painted. It cost me a good deal of money since I had only just hired the painters several months before, but it was worth it to see the back of his flabby body and her perfectly toned one as they and their entourage left with their spoor of chaos trailing behind.

Norman left my house, needing a U-Haul to take all the stuff he and Delilah had accumulated. But strangely enough he did not leave my life. Somehow he managed to convince my chairperson, the well-known Victorianist Samuel Morse, that Norman was one of the major poets of the South Seas. The idea of having a poet working on a cycle of poems about the Maori (Norman let on that he was half-Maori—his father a Jew, his mother a Maori princess, when in fact he was born in Brooklyn to a Hoboken seamstress and a Canarsie tailor) so appealed to the post-colonially minded people in the department that he was made full professor almost overnight, while Delilah got an all-expenses-paid scholarship to study Pacific rim erotics. (I am still not sure if the word "rim" referred to "Pacific" or "erotics.") They felt that they were getting an aboriginal Ezra Pound and his Maori Frida Kahlo. What they got was big trouble, tenured for eternity.

That is the story of my unfortunate affiliation with Norman Goldman. Or was until the phone rang. I picked it up and it was he.

"Bill," he said, using the dimunitive I've shunned all my life, "I've got a favour to ask you." (You could hear the "u" sliding in and just about eliding the Brooklyn diphthong.) "My car just went bust. Could I borrow yours for a few days?"

I have a Volvo station wagon, as do most academics—especially leftists. The cultural reasons for this are too complex and irrelevant to go into here, but suffice it to say that the abhorrence of bourgeois production squeals to a skid in the driveway. I love my car, and I keep it clean. Goldman attracts dirt, lint, dog hair, and newspapers with the force of a Van De Graaff generator. If you are walking on a windy day and run into Goldman, you are likely to see newspapers clinging to his stained trousers. I hate being put into positions where I have to be generous and hate having to be generous to people whom I despise. But I also I hate being shown up as ungenerous.

"For how many days?"

"Just two . . . or three."

"Gee, Norman," I always started to sound incredibly American when I spoke with him, "I'd love to let you, but Anne has to . . . ," I was thinking fast now, " . . . take the kids to the doctor."

"No problem, I'll get them there and then take off."

"Where are you going?" It seemed suddenly as if I had better ask him.

"Manitoba."

"Manitoba," I echoed like an empty rock face.

"Just a quick trip. There and back."

"Going alone?"

"No, someone's coming."

I had to admire the dodge. I tend to feel I must answer all direct questions in full detail.

"Oh . . . "

"So? Would it be better for me to pick it up today or tomorrow?"

"Tomorrow," I said before the millisecond realization that I had fallen into the brilliant negotiating trap he had laid by settling on the secondary issue. By then it was too late.

When Goldman pulled up in my car, after dropping Anne and the children off at the doctor, where they were forced now to go through a routine checkup although no one was sick, I saw in the passenger's seat the face about whom I had really not been thinking.

Christopher sat passive and golden, like a treasure that had been stolen from me. He smiled wanly in what I was not allowed to call betrayal, and the car drove off with a storm of dust that surrounded his head in a nimbus.

When the car was returned, five days later, filled with popcorn crumbs, paper, dog hair, and all the effluvia I had predicted, there was, as I noticed, a dark, brown stain on the passenger side much like the one in my waste basket.

Goldman left me a copy of his most recent book of poems, *Body Rages*. I waited until I got to my office, then I opened to the first poem and read:

FALLEN GIFTS
(*to Christopher*)

My blood in the orange.
My tongue between your teeth.
My sadness in late fall
when the trees know only the bareness
of the empty pines and the desolate
rose with its last icy buds.

Then the gifts of flesh
seem all the more touching
like bow on the cello
and the rasp of rosin

against gut, skin against
bone. The glide of saliva
beading the hard
of the soft. And the soft
of the hard.

> Then we need the ropes and
> accouterments to tie the
> body tight to the short
> days. To tie the meaning
> to the place where the flesh
> meets the bone, and the bone
> meets the gristle. Ligaments
> and life, one torn between the other.
> Where the hard bumps against the hard.
> And the soft pants
> under the weight of the
> cold.

It wasn't Shakespeare. But it wasn't half bad. My first impulse
was to analyze it. But the hard and soft imagery somehow repelled me, and the notion of bondage in the "ropes and accou-
terments" turned me off—particularly when I thought of which
hard or soft things they might be tied to.

Shits like Goldman somehow managed to create beautiful
things. How is that possible that unlike can come from like?
How can a beer-bellied, callous lout produce a golden statue?
This way with words, this glibness, is what attracted legions of
students who followed him with adoring eyes and bodies. How
seducible they were to fall for words arranged on a page. They
would sleep with anything that could arrange them suggestively,
even a computer program. And how could Christopher be one
of them? My interest in him reduced instantly to the kind of
attention one reserves for an ant spied carrying a large grain of
sand on a day of too much sun and too little to do. I saw his
small face in the car like a child going on a weekend excursion
with his father. How could that face seem worthy of admiration
rather than the kind of condescending approval we give the
young because their paucity of experience is absolutely no threat
to our existence?

My interest in him was over.

4

TAKE ALL MY LOVES, MY LOVE,

YEA, TAKE THEM ALL

Life without Christopher was very much like life with Christopher. It was more of a concept gone awry than a being lost. I went about my days, teaching, reading, working on my book. This was a love affair that never happened. So there was not much mourning, and there was no guilt. What had I done but had some silly thoughts really?

Anne and I decided to take a weekend at an inn in a small town in Vermont. We had gone there years before when we were first going out. It was a romantic spot, and perhaps because romance had turned familiar, we both wanted to make it unfamiliar. You could say that the whole incident with Christopher suddenly made me feel that there was a kind of remarkable, audacious knowledge in life that I had allowed slowly, so slowly that I was not aware of the slowness, to turn into the merest of utility.

When we got to the inn, I said to Anne, "Remember the smell here?"

"Mmmmm. Smells like pine tar and roses."

"More like beeswax and mildew."

We were always trying to specify smells, and we never agreed on the other's palate.

"Let's go for a walk," Anne suggested.

"I was thinking of the bed."

"Sleep! On a glorious day like this?"

"I wasn't thinking of sleeping . . . "

"Oh, you!" she said, and punched me as if I were suggesting robbing the bank. "Let's go for a walk, we can always make love later."

It was a small passage of words, and when I write it down, I think it looks fine. But whenever I have that conversation with her something delicate gets crushed in me. A small chanterelle, dark and precociously orange against the forest floor, gets trampled on and never looks the same. Marriage for the middle-aged is always a set of problems in solution or solutions about to complicate themselves into problems. Not that there is not love. Not that the young do not find themselves in the center of tempests of the heart, but the older man sees that nothing can make a defense against time's scythe except desire and work. And work finally is, despite what Carlyle would say, only a consolation. So that leaves desire, which as Freud would say, is always a consolation for some other lost desire.

We went for our walk. It promised to be a beauteous day, so we went out without our raincoats. But quickly dark clouds overtook us on our way.

"Those clouds," I said, "they look like rotten smoke."

"Why 'rotten smoke'?" Anne asked in a practical way.

"Smoke from rotting hay, or maybe smoke from burning plague cadavers."

"Heavens!" she said and shuddered. "You have a bizarre imagination. Do you have to be so perverse. It's just rain clouds."

The rain did not take its time coming, and we found ourselves with storm-beaten faces, dripping with water as if we had been sobbing.

"Let's go back," I said, feeling that the water was a kind of salve. We trudged back to the hotel.

We had to take off our wet clothes, dripping onto the quaint appointments of the room filled with the small, flowered ornaments and the chintz that makes us feel we are really in an inn and not in someone else's house. There were two beds. They were both full-sized beds with identical bedspreads. One was better than the other in some way I could not specify. When I put my arm on Anne's naked body, I wanted to pull her to the second-best bed. Why I am not sure, but that bed seemed better for sex, for lust. She however pulled me toward the other bed, which felt more proper and well made. I let her pull me and slowly descended onto her.

There is that moment when flesh touches flesh. Even if the bodies have felt each other countless times before, the moment reenacts the time those bodies first touched. I closed my eyes and lay still in the warmth of contact. Lying in the better bed with Anne, feeling her arms, legs, torso, breasts not individually with the hands but all at once with the surface of my body was like inhaling champagne. I wanted to keep hold of that feeling, but her hands began to explore my body in known ways, the ways we had developed together over so many years, the way couples might write music together, or bake a cake, so that there is foreknowledge that is at once routine and yet comforting. I too let my hands wander in the familiar journey.

Sex with Anne had always been comforting but always proper. It was always for reproduction. Even before we wanted to have children, it was for reproduction. And now, even after having children, it was for reproduction. Reproduction with birth control is the kind of paradox we both live with and try to understand. Or try to ignore.

Afterward, Anne and I had dinner. It was the kind of dinner menu one does not remember very well later, except for the crinkly shininess of the aluminum foil on the baked potato and the fishy smell that hovered like an olfactory mirage over the

halibut. New England inns often feature quaintness without deft-
ness of quality, in that American way that places virtue on sub-
stance rather than caliber. So over the suggestion of bounty rather
than over bounty itself, we gazed on each other's vacation faces,
relaxed from time and the leisure of making love in the afternoon.

"I wonder how the kids are doing," said Anne.

"They're fine; what could be wrong?"

"Well, a lot could be wrong."

"A lot could always be wrong. But we have to assume that
most of the time things are fundamentally okay."

"That's such a naive view of things," she said, buttering her
roll.

"Why do people always call 'naive' what they don't happen
to believe. Why is it more realistic to be pessimistic?"

"Because things go wrong more often than they go right."

"What do you mean? Look, we are sitting here breathing,
eating. Our cells are working. Oxygen is being exchanged for
carbon dioxide in our corpuscles. Atoms are spinning. Thousands of millions of tiny, complex actions are going right. Isn't
that more right than wrong?"

"Technically, yes," she admitted to my bludgeoning, "but
right now a cancer cell in my breast could be starting to multi-
ply. Right now our kids could be in a fatal car crash."

"Have some tartar sauce," I said.

"Thanks."

"It could cause botulism."

"Ha."

"Are you ever just plain happy?" I provoked.

"Just plain happy? What am I supposed to be . . . someone in
Oklahoma?"

"Well, that might be better than *No Exit.*"

"Is that a criticism? I thought this was a romantic dinner."

"Well, it was supposed to be until you started worrying that
the kids were dead."

"I didn't. I just said I wondered how they were."

"No. You said they might be dead."

She got silent and drew her lips taut in imitation of her Puritan forebears. She suddenly became someone in a Grant Wood painting. When I first met Anne, she was a student at Radcliffe, and I was at Harvard. She was a sociology major. As people said then, "A sosh major." It sounded softer, more radical, like the rumpled green book bags thrown over their shoulders. Her blonde hair was long, and she tended to braid a small bit and make it into an Ophelia-like wreath that delicately crowned her head. She looked for all the world like the essence of an exotic flower child. Anne was the wild, daring person that I was not. She dropped acid with the casualness of dropping her purse. She smoked dope, imploded at various crash pads, had many boyfriends, all of who looked like crosses between Mick Jagger, John Lennon, and Jimi Hendrix. She seemed to provide me a passage, a viaticum, out of my urban cage and to give me a way to live more wildly.

I never thought I would go out with her. But one day there was a takeover of the school. Hundreds of students poured into the administration building. That night we slept in the offices. Anne was next to me, and in the dark of the early morning, without much warning, we were kissing each other on the floor of the Associate Dean for Academic Research's office. As we rolled around, the music of the Grateful Dead murmuring out of someone's portable radio, and the file cabinets towering over us, I felt that a mystery was unfolding.

But Anne really was no Janis Joplin. She only looked like one. I first realized this when I met her parents. They lived in New Canaan. Instead of the interesting poet and writer I had fashioned myself into, I suddenly became the poor, urban boy in one second of conversation. Her parents were from central casting—her father the grey-haired, well-groomed businessman; her mother in her shirtwaist, with understated short hair and clothing from Lord and Taylor; even their dog, an Irish setter, seemed to know about my origins.

"Anne," her father said *sotto voce*, but not *sotto* enough that I could not hear, "are you serious about this boy?"

"Dad!" she said in that defensive, annoyed, angry tone that children of all classes specialize in.

"I'm just asking, dear. No need to get all huffy."

"Kiki," her mother said to her, using the family's nickname, "doesn't Will remind you of someone? That nice boy who you used to bring here?"

Anne knew to expect the other shoe to fall.

"You know, Kiki, the one whose parents owned the dry goods store."

"Are your parents related to the Marlowes of Westport?"

We left as quickly as we could, stealing a few bottles of gin and some choice Bordeaux as we went.

Once college was over, Anne dropped the rebellious stance and quickly assumed the mantle of respectability her family had mail-ordered for her. The beautiful long hair got lopped off. Shirtwaists began to appear. She became a consultant to businesses on improving communications between employees. At that point we broke up, and she married a juvenile clone of her father. They got divorced two years later, and I met her again when I was in graduate school. We got married pretty quickly, realizing that we had really loved each other all along. Ironically, I was drawn to a fantasy of her wildness, but I ended up living her staid, orderly reality. After all, I was not exactly Jimi Hendrix.

Now Anne sat at the table, lips pursed, thinking about the death of our children. What would it take to get her back to those days? I looked at her blue eyes.

"Anne, remember that concert we went to in Hyde Park— the one the Rolling Stones did in memory of the dead drummer? What was his name?"

"Yes, I remember the concert but I . . . what *was* his name? They let all those doves go. They rose up into the sky like a fireworks of feathers."

"Remember how we sat on the roof of someone's Volkswagen van and it collapsed in . . . became inverted?"

She laughed. "That was terrible. I felt so guilty."

"But who cared in those days? No one felt guilty for long."

"I did. I still do. I think of that poor guy coming back from this great concert and seeing his car all caved in."

"Yeah, well . . . "

Those days were clearly over, perhaps they never really were there except as a wish in some people's minds and a blush of druggy remembrance.

On the ride back to New York, Anne did the entire *Sunday Times* crossword puzzle, while I played *Blonde on Blonde* on a continuous loop.

"Nobody feels any pain," Dylan keened as I drove at 3 miles above the speed limit.

5

MY MISTRESS' EYES ARE
NOTHING LIKE THE SUN

I was teaching a graduate course on the sonnets, trying to or-
ganize my ideas for the book on which I was working.
Shakespeare's sonnets have been so extensively discussed it is
hard to think of anything new that can be said about them. My
idea was to teach a course on Queer Theory and Shakespeare. It
was a subject I was not that familiar with, but I had heard
someone say it had become a growth industry. The bisexuality of
the sonnets had really been soft-pedaled in the past. In fact, the
now obvious homosexuality of the poems had rarely been mentioned by the dusty Oxford dons who owned and licensed the
Bard. Sitting in their comfortable studies, these scholars would
twist themselves into amazing contortions by insisting that the
love between Shakespeare and his darling young man was purely
platonic. These might be the same dons who were randily screwing their *Brideshead Revisited* male students. Then of course they
have less trouble acknowledging sex with the Dark Lady, as she
is called, although no one can really figure out what she is about
or who she is. Anyway, my idea was to look at all the work done

by gay, lesbian, bisexual, and transgendered critics and to focus on sex rather than avoid it.

My class was a strange mixture of students, all the stranger because it met at nine in the morning. I only teach morning classes for two reasons. The first is that I get very sleepy in the afternoon, and the second is that I feel that only very motivated students will come to a nine AM class. My theories seem to have been all wrong this year because I was barely able to get up in time for the class and only unmotivated students seem to have appeared. The title of the course, "Queer Theory and the Sonnets," pulled in a diverse lot. There was a middle-aged Jesuit who sat quietly in the back taking copious notes and rarely speaking. Then there was the predictable set of flesh-and-cartilage-pierced students with odd-colored hair, most of whom seem to be coming off of some drug or another from the previous night's partying. There was a woman who had recently come back to academia from business still in the midst of a transition from business suits to jeans. Today she happened to be wearing the business suit jacket and leather jeans, and appeared to be a kind of cultural-studies satyr, civilized above and animal below. And then there was Chantal.

Chantal S. T. Mukarjee was dark in many ways. (The S. stood for Sarah and the T. for Terpsichore.) Her origins were obscure, emerging from a French colonialist grandfather, a Jewish one, and several Greek, Middle Eastern, and subcontinental grandmothers. She was dark. Her eyes were nothing like the sun, and her brows were raven black. Her lips somewhat pale against her skin which was like light sand at the edge of the beach made suddenly dark by the lap of the water. The skin was remarkable for its failure to catch the light or the color, and so her hue was always dark and always secure in its darkness. Her eyes were even darker, like dark-matter that absorbed any possible illumination. The effect was obscure. It was hard at a glance to know what she was thinking or feeling, and yet there were flashes of illumination in the darkness, like bursts of St. Elmo's Fire, that made one see peculiar brilliances.

The first time I saw Chantal in my class, I had to laugh. She was a preposterous dresser and had on a kind of gown that belonged in a Jean Harlow movie. It was black and had long slits up the front revealing her dusky legs. She said it was the rage in Italy. Fine, but not at nine in the morning on a dreary day at Columbia. Clearly, some of the men in the class thought of her as a black Athena. But she was no goddess; she walked on the ground.

That was not really the first time I cast my eyes on her. I had seen her at a concert given by the Renaissance Society. It was a recital of Dowling's songs sung by a rather elongated and somewhat gnarled tenor with a beautiful voice, a graduate student oddly named Gnostril Nosenbaum. Oddly named, as he explained, because his father, a lapsed Jew, had been fascinated by the Gnostic gospels and decided to name his son Gnostel as a synergistic tribute to those texts, but some bleary-eyed nurse, seeing the last name, also ineptly given by an Ellis Island clerk to an unlucky forebear, erred in the direction of consistency of body parts. The song was accompanied on an original instrument. In this sonically correct moment, Gnostril's voice, more fair than fair, issued from a Grecian nose as if it originated there. The voice bloomed into a rose of sound and then exfoliated into the deciduous tinnitus of silence. Meanwhile, around the exquisite tune were the tinkling staccato stabs of the virginal played by none other than Chantal. The virginal, as inaptly named as Nosenbaum was, in effect, aptly named, sat on a *faux* sixteenth-century table, the small, lacquered box grinding out the primitive tunes as the dark fingers danced on the light wooden keys. The jacks popping out of the box nimbly leapt to kiss the tender inward of her hand. She was wearing a sari that looked slinky, vermillion and satin, her dark hair coiled up like an adder poised to strike from the delicate perch of her skull.

I was sitting next to Norman Goldman. Fate always has it that the ones we despise the most are the ones whose company we are doomed to keep. Norman was breathing in his stertorous manner, as usual, and sucking small filaments of food from his yellow teeth. He ran his hands over his odiously greasy hair and leered at me in that way that males do when they wish to imply bonding through the appreciation of a beautiful woman.

"I'd like to be tickled by her fingers. I can tell you where, too! Like those jacks, I would blushing stand, I would."

I tried to ignore his innuendo, concentrating on the willowy harmonics of the tenor's voice, but I had to admit in some form of silent conspiracy with his and my middle-aged climacteric, looking at her sweet fingers, gently swaying, making a concord of music, watching them walking with gentle gait across the keys, that I could have kissed her hand and her lips if there was a remote chance of escaping sexual harassment charges.

"Norman," I said, "you're getting a little old for that!"

"Speak for yourself. I fancy I'll be too old for that when they put me in my bloody coffin. But even then I plan, like the hanged, to die with a hard-on. My death mask will put Dante's to shame. When they ask 'What did that bloody poet look like?' they'll have to answer loudly: 'He was endowed.' " I think he meant his organ and not his chair, to which he had been recently and misguidedly appointed. He was now the Claire Booth Luce Professor of Poetry and Colonial Studies, so successfully had he pulled the New Zealand wool over the eyes of the doddering administration. Meanwhile I remained unacknowledged, occupying a small oak and leather chair that had no name other than that of its manufacturer—the Acme Furniture Company of New Bedford, Massachusetts. I like to think of myself as the Acme Furniture Professor of Shakespearean Studies.

By now, I had had more than enough of Norman's endless song of himself, so I got up and wandered in a seemingly aimless direction to my unacknowledged goal where Chantal sat receiving compliments.

I waited my turn behind the line of admiring men of varying ages and configurations of facial hair. "That was beautifully played," I said somewhat awkwardly. "I don't think Wanda Landowska could have outdone you there."

"You belie me with false compare," she demurred.

"Have you been playing long?" proleptically expecting to hear the answer implied by the question.

"Twenty years. The blink of an eye." She smiled and blinked.

I had expected to hear from her sari-clad person a tinge of an Indian accent or perhaps a European one like the rich wine that should accompany a complex meal. Instead her accent was that of a Wal-Mart shopper. The Dowling was served up with a Diet Pepsi instead of a Haut Brion. She was American as apple turnover. She just looked foreign in some indefinable, cumulative way. Her lips seemed to be Jewish, her cheeks French, her skin Indian, her nose Greek, her eyes Arabic. Her body was thin and elegant, almost African, and her hair was raven black and glossy like a Polynesian's. I thought back to my friend Stephen who had once said that his wife was "all women to him." (He eventually divorced her.) I never understood what he meant until I saw Chantal.

"So, what drew you to this kind of music?" I asked, desperately seeking a topic of conversation.

"It's athletic. I think of Renaissance music as aerobic." She knocked the words off as if she were asking for a sports bra at Macy's.

"Aerobic?"

"Sure. They danced to everything then. Music was either for divine contemplation or for dancing."

"Like Stairmaster," I joked, thinking of Delilah's now departed igneous thighs.

"Yes," she agreed too quickly and without humor. "They were incredibly athletic. Have you ever seen that painting erroneously thought to be Queen Elizabeth dancing with the Earl of Leicester?"

I tried to remember, but nothing appeared in my mind.

"Well, the male dancer is holding the female up in the air. I mean that was athletic. She is held at an arm's length in the air, held up by the busk."

"The busk? That would be the whale-bone that stiffened the corset, wouldn't it?"

"That would be some nobleman holding up his lady by her intimate apparel."

"Yes, well, that would be not only athletic but pretty risque."

"Try it. It's not easy. You'd have to work out."

"Well, I don't."

"I can see that."

"Do you? Work out, that is?"

"Not *even* . . . !" She said that in the best ditzy teenage girl voice she could improvise. "I have to work out everyday. Quadriceps on the machine; fingers and arms on the harpsichord."

I looked at her arms, which were so much more defined and pumped-up than mine. I thought about how we were creating a race of women with the upper-body strength of galley slaves.

"That's remarkable." Everything I said felt stupid and terse. So I stopped talking and just looked at her. My gaze was soft-focused and detailed. She was not beautiful in some classical sense, but that was of course her beauty. Classical looks are predicated on white standards, if you consider the Greeks white. No, she was beautiful in some multicultural sense, which probably was the most universal beauty, by definition, one could find.

"Is that gaze male?" she said watching me watch her.

"Is that remark gendered?"

We were wrestling for the phallus, as Lacan would have said, had he been there. Had he been there, he would have had the phallus, but luckily he was dead, his penis now a dry bit of parchment having lost all claim to lofty signification.

She let her fingers walk on the keys a bit and furrowed her brow. I thought I saw the undulating mirage of heat rise up from the virginal, a smell of musk and rose, a sensation of darkness, of night. I had to leave. The uncomfortable sense of desire marked itself as inappropriate. The bars between faculty and student, between married and unmarried, rose up like a reverse portcullis, and I only nearly escaped simultaneous beheading and impalement.

"Well, good luck in your playing," I said as avuncularly as I could muster. (Although I never talked to my nieces that way.)

The next time I saw Chantal, she was sitting at the seminar table. I remembered with some embarrassment my attraction for her as I shuffled the papers on my desk. It was the first day of class, always a time filled with promise. Students are glossed with a patina of originality and freshness that has not begun to dull with time and observation. To the students, the teacher has not yet become pompous, long-winded, or banal; instead the professor remains frozen for a moment of time before his or her inevitable fall into endless repetition of a single insight developed and refined over time that will either make a career or dissolve it. The moment is like the nuptial instant in a Jewish wedding just before the breaking of the ritual glass. All is crystalline, etched, vitreous. Nothing is shattered.

I spoke about the nature of the course, what would be expected, the theme of queer theory, and its importance in recent years. I had to admit I was new to this material, not being gay or transgendered. I articulated what I recently learned is my "subject position." Students took notes. Chantal appeared to be asleep. Not asleep exactly but sitting with her eyes closed. I could not tell if her stance was one of tedium or simply abstraction.

I asked a general question. Why the sonnet? Why does someone as creative as Shakespeare take a form that is so strictly limited? And why does he return obsessively to this fourteen line straitjacket with its invariable rhyme scheme, fixed three quatrains and an always rhymed last couplet? Why does this man, almost forty, run home every day, or every other day, to write cumulatively 154 sonnets to a young man with whom he is madly in love but who seems to be largely indifferent to Shakespeare. He assembles the most beautiful sonnet sequence ever to a young man who betrays him at every step, whom he betrays, and to a mistress whom he finds alternately ugly and fascinating. Why does he never write a single poem or even a line in a poem to his wife? Why use this sonnet form and not a longer poem? Why does he never use the Italian sonnet with octave and sestet? Why does this man of great originality and inventiveness always return to the sonnet like a dog to his own vomit or like a horse to its stable? Why this lack of originality in these, Shakespeare's only known writings about himself?

As I finished my litany there was the inevitable silence that long, unfocused questions always bring. They hang in the air like a confusing mist, and then drop to the floor like theatrical smoke. The Jesuit looked up from his notebook like a man suddenly awakened by a loud noise. His face was confused. A woman in leather was applying black lipstick to her flaking lips. Because the class did not respond, I began to fill the void with my own thoughts.

"The answer has to be Shakespeare's obsessive fear of death. His sonnets are all about time, about time running out, about how he is getting older and the young man, his lover, is getting older. How do you solve the problem? You write. Writing foils death. And sex foils death—or maybe it is death. So it's all about the relation between sex and death. Shakespeare must have felt his sexual longings as evanescent, as he does in Sonnet 129. The only thing that justifies his existence is love. But the object of his love is aging too. Shakespeare tries to freeze time by writing sonnets. Sonnets are these little, perfect forms. Little songs, is the literal meaning. These poems are like small treasure chests, or perhaps coffins, in which he can lock his love, his body, the lover's body.

"Think of this. Shakespeare is about thirty-eight. He is a somewhat successful playwright. He is married to Anne Hathaway. He has children. He splits his time between London and Stratford. In London, he dines, he drinks, he revels. Then he returns home to Stratford with Anne. Could his life there hold a candle to London? Perhaps this marriage suits them both. He can cavort in London and return to a rural retreat. Or perhaps his is a marriage of convenience. He is really gay; perhaps she is a lesbian. He indulges in women from time to time, but his love for women is really lustful, just fucking." I paused here to let the vulgarity sink in; to let my and their embarrassment evaporate a bit. "But with men, there is love. There is the ideal. There is something noble and

beautiful. Here he finds the combination of passion and devotion."
I thought of Christopher for one brief second.

Gnostril Nosenbaum's hand went up.

"I have a thought," he said with his beautiful tenor voice now
simply a strangely high-pitched speaking voice. "Is there anything
in Shakespeare's life that would lead us to think of lemurs?"

"Lemurs?" I echoed, "I'm not sure. Why do you ask?"

"Well, lemurs are related to monkeys, and they are noctur-
nal. They are found mainly in Madagascar."

"I'm missing your point."

"You see, there is enough evidence to speculate that
Shakespeare might have been aware of lemurs since trade had
been going on with India and the East. Lemurs, not being exactly monkeys, might have been a kind of missing link between
humans and primates, if you see what I mean."

"I really don't," I said, trying to steer the conversation back
to the sonnets, but Gnostril plowed on.

"We know that Shakespeare does mention monkeys and apes
several times in his work, when for example he says in *Timon of
Athens* 'The strain of man's bred out into baboon and monkey.'
You see a kind of reverse evolution. I mean, it is thought by
some experts that Caliban might be based on an account of a
missing link, possibly a lemur described by some explorer. Interesting, isn't it?"

No one nodded.

"But, it just occurred to me that lemurs are possibly mentioned in the sonnets. And I have noticed a number of places
where lemurs seem to be alluded to in the sonnets. For example,
in the last sonnet, 154, the 'little Love-God' could in fact be a
lemur."

"Mr. Nosenbaum, this is fascinating and would no doubt make
a wonderful paper. May I suggest you write up your thoughts?"

He appeared to want to say more, but at that moment
Chantal's eyes opened briefly, flickered open really like a slightly
askew doll that has been righted. She raised her hand.

"Yes, um . . . " I looked at my list of students' names although I knew hers perfectly well. "Um . . . yes . . . Ms. Mukarjee."

"To return to your question, the form of the sonnet was well established. Invented by Petrarch, I think. It was old technology, really. Wyatt, Surrey, Spenser—they all wrote them. Then Shakespeare was working on his plays. Well, that was new stuff. Really different from the revenger tragedies, all those bodies littering the stage—rape, poking out of eyes, and all that. So Shakespeare was working all day with this new stuff. It was like cyberspace would be now. But when he wanted to write about his sexual attraction, his desire, he went back to the sonnets. They were old technology. He says as much in Sonnet 72."

Nosenbaum raised his hand again, but I tried to ignore it.

"So what do you make of that?" I asked. "Why go back?"

"Why? Isn't it obvious?" she asked provocatively, but then went on to answer. "It's really rather simple if you take a materialist point of view. Say you work all day on a computer; you're going to write your love letters on a nice piece of stationary with ragged edges. Or if you are going to blow up a building, you don't write your letter on a laser printer, but you cut out those letters from the magazines."

"I'm losing you here," I said.

"It's the phallus," she said matter-of-factly.

"It's the lemur," Nosenbaum managed to interject for a split second before I came back with my own retort.

"Lacan's or Shakespeare's?"

Gnostril looked confused and Chantal made a kind of "duh" face at me that I recognized from my daughter's repertoire of sarcastic visual communications.

"My opinion is that Shakespeare saw his new plays, his whole new technology of drama, as essentially clitoral in nature. He was taking apart the hegemonic male tradition of the revenger's plays. Kyd, Marlowe—were all incredibly phallic, about penetration, mutilation, rape, incest. I mean it was a man's world on that stage. And Shakespeare broke down the Law of the Father with his clitoral counterhegemonic deconstruction of drama."

"Wait," I said, coming up for air. "How could you say that Shakespeare was clitoral? I mean a lot of people see him as promoting the whole male-dominance thing." I wasn't going to be out-feminated by this mere graduate student.

"Ah, yes, well that would be how a generation of old-style feminists might see it, but we need some cultural relativity here." She smiled and batted her long eyelashes. "You see, Shakespeare is a male-chauvinist pig. No question. But, at the time, his work was clitoral compared to what came before (no pun intended). You see, that's why he went back to the sonnets—they were traditional, therefore phallic."

Another tall woman in jeans, with salt and pepper hair, raised her hand.

"Yes, Jean." I said.

"This is a ridiculous discussion," Jean pounced. "Shakespeare is the guy who brought you the classic stereotypes . . .women-as-evil-villainess-bitches or pure-sweet-things. How could he be doing a clitoral reading? The guy was a major prick."

"There might be more in this than meets the eye," Nosenbaum darted in his opinion. "I mean primatology might offer us some insight."

Chantal looked angrily at Gnostril. "Gnosey, back off this lemur stuff. This is all we get twenty-four seven." His crest fell. She turned to me. "He thinks everything in creation can be explained by the ontological position of the lemur." Then to Jean, "I'm not saying Shakespeare wasn't sexist. I'm only saying that formally, culturally, he was in a feminized relationship to his times. He was presenting women as more complex. Where else would you get a Lady Macbeth or a Beatrice? Certainly not in those head-slicing, *Terminator II* plays of the Elizabethan period. And forget the mystery plays, they were even worse. Anyway, my point is that he went back to the phallic sonnets as a way of devolving to a simpler technology—against the 'new-found methods' he talks about in Sonnet seventy-six. He went to get the phallus. This is the true bisexuality of Shakespeare."

"I'm not sure I'm following you," I said. I could see the other students getting impatient with Chantal's wheel spinning. Gnostril's hand was perpetually up, and now began to look more and more like a monkey's arm reaching for a tendrilous vine. I wanted to stop the one-way conversation and let the others give their opinions. But, aside from Gnostril's ape version of literary history, they had no opinions. Not like hers. There was something compelling in what she said. Of course, she was wrong. Of course, she overgeneralized. I had to show her that there were standards to thought. She couldn't just go on like that. But deep within me a grudging admiration rose like a bubble from the place in the ocean where light never arrives. I felt like a lantern fish who had been carrying around my dim, dangling light and is suddenly blinded by the brightness of burning phosphorus.

"You see, Shakespeare is both clitoral and phallic. He is clitoral in his drama, and he is phallic in his sonnets. But that is paradoxical because in his sonnets he lets himself become feminized. He is in a passive subject position begging his young man to come to him, crying when he doesn't. So it is the phallic tradition of the sonnets, his attempt to get the phallus, that lets him become a woman."

A bright young man with small, oval horn-rimmed glasses and a black denim jacket spoke up through his goatee. "I think these observations of Chantal's are a bit dangerous. There is something deeply problematic with these postmodern explanations. Interventions like these could be devastating if they continued to be expressed."

"Devastating?" I asked.

"Yes," he continued quietly with the kind of intensity. "She is suggesting a universality to history. It doesn't matter if Shakespeare lived in the past or now. You see, this explanation lacks a material base. If this explanation is universal, then no one can change anything. There is no possibility of agency. I think we have to consider how class fits into this analysis. Does the lower class have the power? Is Shakespeare's phallus really his or is this just an obscuring way of forgetting about money and oppression?"

Chantal shot back, "I consider myself a Marxist, if that's what you mean. But don't you realize that Marx was a man. He was male. His is only one story. There are many stories, all dependent on each other . . ."

The young man leapt in. "But, are you saying that Marx is wrong? That's such a bourgeois assumption. Look at you in your dress, with your social privilege. Why don't you examine your own subject position that allows you to elide the plight of the poor and the oppressed."

I knew better than to say, "What does this have to do with Shakespeare?" In the millennial classroom, huge stakes depend on small textual matters. Instead I announced that we were out of time. The young man and Chantal glowered at each other like strikers and scabs across a police barrier.

The period was over, and the class filtered out. Nosenbaum immediately came up and began to talk.

"Did you know that the word *monkey* actually has a literary origin. It comes from a character in *Reynard the Fox*. The son of Martin the Ape is called *Moneke*."

"That's fascinating," I said as I caught a glimpse of Chantal leaving. I saw her annoyed face and then a flash of black hair against the black dress. I felt like a wounded man. It wasn't just that she was smart, oddly beautiful, and talented. There was a kind of exuberant, obnoxious confidence that issued forth like hungry hounds being let out of a kennel. My personality was different, less excited, less excitable. More like cats as they hesitate at the door and weigh the possibility of stepping outside.

I thought about Shakespeare's life as I walked down 116th Street and turned onto Riverside Drive. It was twilight. The wind was up, but the apple-wine taste of autumn was still among the trees mixed yet with the sweetness of summer. The last lights of the day were streaming through the polluted air, and the full star that ushers in the evening seemed to turn only half that glory to the sober west. I said hello to the doorman and waited for the elevator. The smell of burnt roast beef filled the hall. I felt an overwhelming sorrow, as if I were going into a cage to be locked up for the night. The walls of the building began to close in like those sinister cells in old Flash Gordon movies when Flash was trapped by Ming from Mongo. The walls closed in, and then water began to fill up the room, slowly at first, then inevitably. I gasped for breath as I opened the door to my apartment, the voices of the children spiraling like double helixes around my head.

6

Mine eye and heart are at mortal war

A new day. I went shopping at Zabar's. Usually there are at least five old men behind the smoked fish counter. They all used to be Jewish. Now they are Asian. I took my number from the dispenser and stared around at the flux of humanity washing from bagels to Dijon mustard and back like an ebbing and flowing tide of gastronomic desire. I never come to this counter without experiencing all the Proustian sensations of my childhood, standing low at my mother's side, her wood and satin handbag dangling next to me. I would look up at the fat men, the array of fish, the pickles in barrels, and be secure that all was right in the world. Now, I glanced at the bounty of whitefish with skins glinting brass, the onyx bubbles of caviar, the damp, coral sides of lox, and the briny, bounding sea rolling over the deeps of pickled herring. I looked up, in the thrall of childhood, as a sirenic voice called out my number. It was Chantal rubbing haunches with the Chinese lox slicers.

"Sixty-five," she said with that flattened voice of American consumer culture.

A woman bedecked in animal furs and crowned with feathers, a woman reeking of overpriced perfume, a woman with makeup more appropriate to carnival than quotidian shoved in front of me and waved her ticket before Chantal's ebony eyes. I lurched forward thinking that no strong hand could hold my swift foot back or forbid me this spoil of beauty. I cried out, "*I'm sixty-five*," as I glared at the female Hun cloaked in her furry armor. Strangely, we both had the same number printed in the same black ink. Whether it was chance, cruel fate, or the eventual randomness of nature that handed me and her the same number, I did not care. I was determined to be served by Chantal and Chantal alone.

"Let me see that," I scowled in spondees, snatching her ticket from her gloved hand. The two tickets were identical. I bluffed.

"You found an old one. Yours has sawdust on it from the floor."

The woman blushed around the edges of her thick layer of makeup. I had found her out. She had stooped her swollen gams to cheat, and I had stooped to conquer. But she persevered in her fib.

"I did not! But if you are going to be so rude, go ahead of me, sir!" She added the final syllable as a mark of condescending triumph.

Sinking from moral high to low ground, I nevertheless decided to snatch my pyrrhic victory from the fish-lipped maw of death. I looked up at Chantal standing in a long white apron that had smears of lox oil arranged in random patterns apparently swirled in Brownian motion.

"Professor Marlow, it's you," she said as she hovered over the shimmery sable, the scent of smoke, fish, brine, and vinegar in the air.

"What are you doing here?" I responded.

"I work here. You can't expect me to make a decent living as a graduate student." I could see it would be difficult to maintain her sartorial splendor on pennies a week. She leaned forward confidentially, "Sometimes it is a little embarrassing. I mean my students come in here and ask me for gefilte fish. Imagine, they say, 'Ms. Mukarjee, two pounds of potato salad.'"

"I can imagine." I did not want to say, "A pound of nova, and make sure there are no bones." So I said, "You know, what you said about the Lacanian phallus yesterday was very interesting." The Hun in furs pressed against my flanks to encourage me to speed up.

"I can't talk about Lacan here."

"I understand."

"No, you don't. It has to do with class."

"My class."

"No, social class. When I'm here, I'm more in touch with the working classes. And you know they are not talking about Lacan. Right, Carl?" She turned to the wizened Asian man next to her who was deftly slicing up a salmon into micron-thin curls. He turned and cracked his austere face into a warm, toothless grin that suddenly made him resemble a gecko. "No lackin'," he whispered back.

"So what'll it be?" she asked me.

"Just the nova."

"How much?"

"Two pounds and . . . "

"Yes?"

" . . . and . . ."

There was something tyrannous, some way her heart was tormenting me with disdain, that was poised with the point of her knife against the naked belly of the salmon. I had caught her working at this menial occupation, and I should have been scorning her, but instead she appeared to be the one doing the scorning.

" . . . and . . . " I couldn't say "no bones." So I trailed off, to the amusement and triumph of the fat woman in furs at my neck, whose perfume was leaking down from her feathered crown onto my shoulders and beyond.

I watched as Chantal exfoliated the salmon from its dull skin and pulled out the bones, as she clearly knew how to do, with needle-nosed pliers. Then she sliced through its body, but I felt as if the body were mine so that I groaned. She looked up and stared. I wanly returned the smile. I was caught, hooked I should say. My eyes could not wrest free of her face, but my heart had begun to waver.

"I'm very interested in food," she said to keep the silence at bay, perhaps. "I have another job."

"Really? What is it?"

"I cook food for the condemned."

I knew there had to be some silver lining to the return of the death penalty to New York State, but until this moment I had not known exactly what it was.

"You get to cook special meals for people on death row. Only for those about to die. They can get anything they want."

"I thought they usually went for McDonalds and Pizza Hut and beer."

The Hun gave me a shove and then sighed audibly. I ignored her, and she actually moved away to try and insinuate herself into another line.

"That's a myth. The problem has been that usually they request those things because they haven't had the opportunity to learn about really good food. So a consortium of gourmet food stores, including Zabar's, is providing a grant to educate the condemned so that their final selection will be more rewarding to them."

Under her direction, the sliced nova piled themselves up in sequence on a waxed paper and then found themselves enveloped in another printed paper, taped, labeled, and priced. It was a miracle of organization, like watching a film running backward as a package spills onto the floor and then reverses so that the spilled material leaps up on the table and wraps itself.

"But I thought you were *for* the working classes? This seems kind of elitist. Anyway, what does it matter what your last meal is going to be?"

"That's when it matters the most!" she shot back. "Why does anything matter? Remember, 'Reason not the need. The basest beggars are in the poorest things superfluous.'"

King Lear, I thought automatically. Then I noticed there were tears in her eyes. "It's because the working classes and the underclasses live lives of broken promises, lack access to all things, are trapped in wage labor and legitimation schemes that they never eat the kind of food that all of the spoiled, pampered bourgeois liberals here eat." The Hun, now terrorizing a neighboring line, turned around in annoyance and scowled. "You think it's frivolous to eat *foie gras,* truffles, and pheasant for a last meal, but *you* drink champagne and go to Le Cirque for your special celebrations. Wouldn't you go to the best restaurant in New York if you knew it was your last meal?" Chantal asked.

She had a point. Carl thought so too, and he cracked his gecko grin at us again. I wanted to stay and talk longer. To find out how she served the meals to convicts on death row. I felt as though I might like to try and commit some capital crime in the hopes of being served by her. But people were lining up behind me and jostling each other in the frenzied desire for smoked fish. They were like people seeking work in the Depression, milling around the factory gates. They were like the hungry at a Red Cross dispensary. Loaves of bread were being hurled to them, as they pressed in a crush down on me. They were the outward embodiments of my own desire, pressing in a frenzy toward Chantal, who stood in her white apron like a priestess at a temple of Aphrodite, like the Madonna of Misericordia with hundreds gathered under her capacious robes. It might be food; it might be fish; it might be the Last Supper—but I saw in a moment of clarity that it was Chantal.

"Anything else?" she asked.

How could I answer that question when the answer was something like, "Yes, please give me everything. I'll take your eyes first, dark somnambulistic vortexes pulling me toward you like a condemned man to his last meal. Then I'll have five bottles of your vital fluids. A pound of your flesh, a bag of your thoughts, ground for drip filter. Slices of your heart. 'Yes' to your lips. Deep draughts from your nipples. Mine eye's due is thine outward part, and my heart's right thine inward love of heart. I'll just take everything. Wrap it up."

But I said, "No thanks. That's fine," and I tried to convey the rest in a world-embracing and meaningful smile that came out simply as a smile like any other smile. She nodded back. The encounter was over.

That night I had a dream. I was in a fruit and vegetable store that was strangely large, empty, and tiled in white. It was owned by Greeks. A few Greek women were buying vegetables from some other women. Then bouzouki music began to swell over the scene. The women began to dance slowly, then, as the tempo picked up, faster and faster. They began to look blacker, thinner, and suddenly like figures on a Mycenaean vase. The white-tiled brightness filled with dark women dancing until the whole scene was a revelry of elongated figures and runes given over to Terpsichor. I stood on the sidelines smiling, and woke up laughing.

7

WHEN IN DISGRACE WITH
FORTUNE AND MEN'S EYES

I stood at the window and kept opening and closing the window lock. It takes time to notice what beautiful things those locks are, that look like ears on their side, that artfully fit into the small, arched glottis on the upper part of the window. I slid the ear part into the glottis and then opened it. Then I slid the ear part out. And did this for what seemed like several hours. Locked, unlocked, locked, unlocked. I had time.

I was looking out on Riverside Drive and on the Hudson River. How many seasons had I looked out to see the ebb and flow of the estuary, the changing sky, the trees in glorious leaf or barren despair? Forty winters had besieged my brow, and in forty more I'd end up in the front of a procession of cars with their headlights on slowly prowling up the Drive.

Death came thick about me like a blanket impregnated with cholera germs. I felt an old and familiar panic rise up that grasped my organs one by one with a chill of the last moment of life. I had been terrified of death since I was a child. When I was seven I overheard a conversation of two older children. They were talking about a prophet who had predicted the end of the world. The Apocalypse was coming soon. They saw my terrified look. The older girl took me on her lap and told me not to worry. I would die so quickly that I would never know what had occurred. This reassurance was like a chilling draft of horror. I would never know. It would just happen. I saw the end of my days. I was lying on a bed. This would be my last moment. I look with dim eyes. I am going to end. There will be no more "I" to say "I" am dying. Everything I have ever done, thought, felt— erased in that moment without the good grace to leave a palimpsest. Every act of good or bad, everybody including my parents, my wife, my children will cease at that moment to exist, to ever have existed. And I cannot will to live. Something great, cruel, and arbitrary says I must turn off with the pomp and ceremony of a wall switch extinguishing a ceiling light.

As I grew up, I could only think this thought. Death was always before me, even in my childish moments of joy. Death was a *basso continuo* to anything I might experience. When I looked at a beautiful woman, I saw a skeleton; a beautiful face, a skull. When I listened to music, I thought about the fact that the composer was dead. As I got older I realized that even though art was immortal, the earth was not. The sun would burn out in some millions of years. Human life and everything unique and special about it would come to an end and the eerie coldness of space would carry on with its background radiation and entropic certainty. And even art would not last. Nothing really does. Everything is that tired tale told by some idiot who thinks his story is full of sound and fury.

As I stood sliding ear into glottis, I plunged into sweet silent thought. I had to sigh about the lack of many things. To many I was successful, certainly. A professor at Columbia, author of three modest books sometimes referred to in other scholars' articles, married to an upstanding wife, father of two anatomically correct children. On the verge of perhaps becoming Chair of the Department, if certain tiresome people either died or retired. I thought some precious friends were gone; my life has not been without sadness, and yet . . .

The doorbell rang. I had to admit I hoped it might be Christopher, I'm not sure why, since I had not thought much about him since his excursion with Norman. As I said, not many people drop by unexpectedly. As I walked to the intercom, I thought that all losses are restored and all sorrows end.

I wanted the voice to be Christopher's; instead it was Chantal's.

"Chantal," she said, and I said, "Come up."

She was wearing a black winter coat and a dark scarf. She had a series of diamonds on her ear in a row like Orion's belt, and a large diamond in her nose. Today she looked very Indian. When she took off her coat, she was wearing a short-sleeved baby tee and denim bell bottoms. Her hair was slicked back rather elegantly. Anne had gone out with the kids, but I had a nervous sense that they would be back soon.

"What can I do for you?"

"I'm sorry to bother you at home, but . . . "

"That's all right. I was just . . . "

She looked around at the oriental rugs, the antiques, and the paintings. "This is a really nice place."

"Well, Columbia housing. There are some perks . . . "

"They always give the professors the big front apartments that face the river. Mine is one that would make Raskolnikov feel he was living in a condo."

"Actually, I always liked his room. He could open the door while lying in bed. That just seemed so convenient."

"Easy for you to say," she muttered under her breath. I mean, I *think* she said that. I felt as though my apartment had large lettering on the walls that said "Bourgeois lackey, capitalist running dog."

"Pardon?" I asked.

"That's all right. You were saying?"

"I forget."

"Raskolnikov's convenient digs."

"Oh, right, well when I grew up in my working-class household I didn't even have a bedroom of my own. I would have loved to have had a small room like his. Luxury." I was pulling out my lower-class credentials. She probably came from some deep-dish, American suburb or some palace in Lucknow.

"I've actually come to ask you a favor," she said changing the subject abruptly.

"Please sit down."

She took her scarf off and sat on the edge of the chair. As she put her foot forward, I could see there was a tatoo on her ankle. It was some kind of a hieroglyph, symbol, or rune I could not quite make out. It looked like an animal but none I had known. I wanted to look, but I felt I should not.

"Well, this is a bit odd. A bit difficult to explain."

I smiled and waited nervously. Was she going to ask me something *outré*? Something that was close to what I would ask her if I had world and time enough?

"You heard me play the virginal."

I nodded.

"Well, I was going for a Ph.D. in music before I switched to literature. I'm still fascinated by music, and now I am composing a series of pieces for the early keyboard in the manner of Heinrich Hündt. These are pieces he would have written if he had lived a little longer. His dates were 1579 to 1609. He was a talented composer for the keyboard, as perhaps you know. His music is rarely performed now, although Salzburg had a festival of his work a few years ago, since he was a native son."

I had never heard of Hündt, but I felt as if I should have. So I kept a small, mysterious smile on my face and nodded beneficently.

"The interesting thing about Hündt was that he was blind from birth, yet he wrote music. You know, philosophers were always wondering what colors were like to the blind or what sounds were like to the deaf."

"Yes, but surely there was nothing unusual about what sounds were like to the blind."

"Right, except that Hündt decided to make a series of musical portraits. He thought of music as a form of painting with sound. A very unusual notion for the sixteenth century, since the first program music came along with the Romantics. In fact, it has been suggested that Beethoven got the idea for his Pastoral from Hündt's 'Arcadian Landscape Threatened by Storm.'

"Sir Joshua Reynolds acknowledged that Hündt's notion of painting with music was valid and wrote a critique of 'Arcadian Landscape' as if it were an oil painting."

"I'm afraid I'm not following what you . . ."

"Oh, sorry. I could go on and on about this because it is a project I've been working on for years." She paused dramatically to make it seem as if she were older than her less than thirty years. "Anyway, Hündt decided to do a series of portraits, but he would do them in music. He was inspired by the idea of portraiture. He'd heard about Dürer's work. Hündt did several portraits—one of the Earl of Leicester, one of Erasmus, and perhaps one of Shakespeare, but this last one seems to have been lost. When he died, most of his work was lost."

I nodded sadly for the loss of this eccentric blind man while I was wondering what she could possibly be getting at. Anne was due to return any minute. Of course, this was a perfectly harmless chat, but I usually did not entertain female students at my apartment. Chantal looked at the liquor cabinet. I looked at her looking. So I had to say,

"Can I get you something?"

"Just some Bushmill's—straight up will be fine."

I poured myself one too, just to keep her company.

"So you want to continue these musical portraits?"

"Yes, and here is where you come in, if I may ask you a favor. I think your face would be perfect."

"Perfect?" I looked behind her in the mirror that reflected my face. Many things had been said about it, but perfect was not one of them. I had a distinguished nose, is how I would like to put it, while others have called it prominent. There were lines under my eyes that were darkened by pigment, and my skin bore the aftereffects of a strenuous case of adolescent acne.

"Yes," she said. "I hope I'm not embarrassing . . . "

"Not at all," I said, embarrassed.

"You see, you have an incredible resemblance to the Earl of Leicester."

I was trying to get used to being the spitting image of the Earl of Leicester.

"The young Earl," she added kindly in response to my doubts.

"But . . . but . . . " I was stammering now. "But wait. I don't understand how you can do a musical portrait in the first place. How could one possibly make a resemblance?"

"Well, this is the incredible thing. This is my secret work, really. My master's thesis." She acted as if she were showing me a new toy. "There was a way. That is why I need to be exact, why I need a real face, a resemblance. I am talking about a three-dimensional image, not just a photograph. You see, Hündt had developed this incredible system, which I think no one besides him has really understood. He wasn't interested in making a melody that would evoke a person, although all musicologists have thought of his portraits that way, kind of tone poems. No, Hündt had a way of actually making a kind of visual representation out of musical notes. It was more accurate than a photograph. You see, I think it was more like a hologram. This was a new technology of music using the keys of the instrument as if they were computer keys."

She had finished her drink, and so had I mine. She took the bottle and poured another. So did I.

"So are you saying that these portraits were . . . visible?"

She took a deep swig and said "Exactly! Visual."

"But how could that be?"

"I believe that Hündt developed a system by which individual notes actually corresponded to spatial locations on a three-dimensional grid which he marked by the positions of his fingers. You've seen the grids that Flemish Renaissance artists used to draw perspective with?"

"Yes, I think so." I could feel the whiskey bringing a resinous warmth to my stomach and its outlying regions.

"They were wooden frames strung with string or wire into grids. The artist simply had to copy what she saw through the squares onto gridded paper and so—reality! Well, Hündt using the same method would mentally grid someone's face. Without seeing, he would feel the subject's face with his hands and note the specific location of each finger through musical notation. Sharps would indicate rising lines; flats falling locations. Key would be used to create different planes, and the whole piece of music, while harmonious itself, was actually an encoded pattern of information. Not only that, but because music moves through time, the picture moves. This is not a three-dimensional picture but a four-dimensional one."

"It moves?"

"Like film. It moves through time. The music is a transcription of Hündt's hands moving over the subject's face as the subject moves through space."

"Incredible," I had to say with the only fitting cliche available. "But is there any evidence, any corroborating evidence, for your interpretation of Hündt's method?"

"Well, in Shakespeare's plays there are many references to music, and some of these link touch to sound." She pulled out a notebook and began to riffle through the pages. "Listen to this. *The Merchant of Venice:* 'if they but hear a trumpet sound, or any air of music touch their ears,' act five, scene one, line 76 or 'with sweetest touches.' " She stopped to make sure I got the reference then continued, "Pierce your mistress' ear and draw her home with music,' act five, scene one, line 68. You see! Or in *Pericles,* 'You are a fair viol, and your sense the strings; Who finger'd to make man his lawful music . . . ' " She seemed delighted with her examples. Then she looked at me.

"Do you realize what this might mean?"

"Yes," I said, stunned. "Three-dimensional moving images of Shakespeare, Queen Elizabeth . . ."

"Right! That is why I need to test my theory. If I can write a piece of music using this system and using your face, it should sound sort of like the one he wrote to portray the Earl of Leicester."

"How would you do that?"

"Well, I'm not sure. I'd have to work on it a bit. Shall I try? Now?"

Without waiting for an answer she got up, closed her eyes, and touched my forehead with her fingers. She would stop for a second, write down a series of notes on a musical score, and then continue. At first her touch was a shock to me. Her fingers were warm with her enthusiasm. They touched my brow lightly. I was tense but began to relax. I felt as if I were being read, being recorded, by her fingers. She moved slowly from my brow to my eyes, then to my nose. She felt every small area of my face. Her fingers came to my lips, and she explored the curve to the nose, the indentation that has no name between the nose and lip, the underlip, the part medical classifiers call the "vermillion border of the lip," the moist surface, the puckers in the corner. Her hands were beginning to consume me, to get more from me than I wanted to give away. Slowly, lightly, delicately, they flitted to my ears, down my neck to my collar bone. This was seduction by pure touch. But it was more than simple seduction, it was violation. I was being taken, drained, and then transcribed.

My response was male. I wanted to kiss her fingers, to feel her face. Touch breeds intimacy far quicker than intimacy breeds touch.

The door opened. Anne and the children walked in.

"Oh dear!" Anne said, reaching into her New England lin-guistic reticule and finding the apt euphemism to comment on what she saw. The children stared the solemn stare of young innocents betrayed. Chantal looked over at them and said, "Hi!"

Anne ushered the children into their room with a shove, as my daughter asked if Daddy had a headache, and that was why the woman was rubbing his head. My son knew better and said nothing.

When Anne returned I said, "Anne, this is Chantal. She has an amazing theory."

Anne looked coldly on this revelation. "I'm sure she has. So do I."

Tedious explanations and hurt feelings followed. Chantal took her notes and left. I had to explain Hündt, the musical portraits, Shakespeare, and so on. It sounded like a tissue of lies into which Lust had blown his nose. Anne left me to my own ruminations, and she packed her bags. She had been planning to visit her folks in New Canaan, and suddenly this seemed like the perfect time.

"I just don't believe you," she said.

"There is an explanation, if you just let me . . . "

"I've let you, and frankly this is preposterous. I'm giving you a week to think about what is important to you. I assume you will not see this woman again, at least you won't if you want to stay married to me."

"But . . . " I hung on the single word. Anne walked out with the children, who cast Orpheus-like looks over their shoulders as the door slammed. Minutes later I heard the Volvo utter its plaintive, somewhat Swedish, bleep several stories below and disarm itself for human entry. I was shocked at the rapidity of this abandonment.

Why did she leave me so quickly? It was as if her bags had been packed for several years. Perhaps they were. I wondered if Anne had a lover that I never knew about, and she was using this ridiculous incident as a pretext for leaving me. I thought of her long, languorous conversations with Ralph Burkhardt, the expert on German *lieder,* or was it the games of tennis on Friday nights with Arthur Kaplan, the mixed doubles that she attended to with an avidity I attributed to the Protestant ethic? Even Norman crept in as a possibility. Had his hypnotic mantra drawn her too into its not-so-subtle flame? Or was it just her incredible sense of justice—an iron ruler inscribed with "Thou shalt not" rammed up her spinal cord by her Puritan forebears? These, after all, were the people who brought the world the Salem witch trials. I could imagine the discussion of my transgressions held at the family compound—the inevitable fall of the lower classes, the predictability of alliances with the cruder sort. I had to take a walk.

I went out into the night air. The cold was so intense it was sadistic. I did not seem to be aware of much besides my confusion. I walked down Broadway and watched the neighborhoods change. Somehow it was 2 AM and I was standing at the Battery, gazing at the Statue of Liberty. New York Harbor led the way out to the Atlantic, filled with icebergs and insensate death. If I swam I could fade into the nothingness that hung like a frayed hem over the rising mists of the ocean. If I did the crawl and the sidestroke long enough I would survive. I would swim forever and eventually come to England, where an even damper cold grips their new dawn. I would crawl ashore, rise naked from the ground, my clothes eaten off by fish and barnacles, and the sunlight pouring golden raiment around me. The church bells would sound seven times; a small ball rolls toward my feet, and young school girls with blue overcoats laugh, avert their eyes, and retrieve the ball. The girl with the ball looks shyly at me and runs away. I might find some clothes in a dustbin and walk from the beach to the grassy lands, and then continue my trek into the green hills, following the winding river. Tracing its way to the Midlands, I would follow it to Stratford-Upon-Avon. My beard having grown long by now, the villagers would gather around in amazement at the haggard stranger. A woman named Anne would take pity on me and bring me into her thatched-roof house. I would lie in her second-best bed in a feverish sweat. In my delirium I hear the children running about. She'd call them. "Hamnet, stop making noise. Tell Susanna and Judeth to keep quiet. He is ill."

"Will he die?" a small voice asks.

"I do not know. Let us pray."

And then one day the fever clears. I open my eyes and see Anne, the good wife, the faithful one who waits eternally. She thinks she knows me now, and she shaves me with a long razor and a bowl full of hot water. And when she finishes, she towels my face and gasps. "It is you," she says with a rueful grin. "You have returned."

"Yes," I say, with tears dropping from the dimness of my recollections. "Yes, I remember now. It all comes back. I have returned." We make love as the children sleep, as if it had all happened before, many times.

As my strength grows, I get up for short intervals. One day, as the sun slants down on the wide floor boards, I rise with a shaky step and walk over to the small, deal desk. With quavering hand, I pick up the quill, dip it in the ink and write in small, cramped letters the word "Sonnets."

8

THE EXPENSE OF SPIRIT IN A WASTE OF SHAME

I was alone beweeping my outcast state when the phone rang. It was Chantal.

"I'm really sorry . . ."

"That's okay. It wasn't your fault."

"But, it was . . . I'm sorry. Did it . . . ?"

"She left. I really couldn't explain. It was so preposterous."

"I wasn't trying to be preposterous!"

"No, not you. *It* was so impossible to explain. It just sounded like I was lying."

"She left you? Just for that . . . For Hündt?"

"It wasn't just that. And she didn't leave me; she just left. For a week. She was supposed to go anyway. This just pushed it."

"Can I make it up to you?" Chantal asked.

"No . . . it's fine." I remembered Anne's prohibition. I just wanted to get off the phone.

"Please, let me do something for you. I am cooking tonight."

"No, I'm sorry. I couldn't have dinner with you."

"No, not me. I'm cooking for the condemned . . . at Sing Sing. Perhaps you could accompany me. It would be interesting and . . . " She stopped to choose her words. " . . . it could be . . . uh . . . redeeming."

Redemption. Yes, I was ready for redemption.

"Let me think about it."

I called her back after a while. Why not? I thought. Anyway, it was a way of seeing her.

A limousine provided by Zabar's picked us up and took us to Sing Sing. The prison rose out of the Hudson Valley like a bad dream. Its hideous architecture was most definitely not evocative of Piranesi. It was more like Mussolini. And the bars on each window made a brief, summarizing statement about the limits of vision and the punitive nature of metal. I thought of my window onto the Hudson; its expansive view and the promise that each sunset held. How much color could be drained out of a life because of a single, transgressive act? I thought of Chantal's hands on my face, and I blushed. What was I doing in prison with her, when Anne had forbidden me to see her at all? What would this explanation sound like? "Sorry Anne, I did see her. No it wasn't a date; we went to prison together." Some story.

Chantal was wearing a pair of blue jeans and a striped shirt under a large tweed overcoat. She looked strangely small and waif-like against the elephantiasis of the prison architecture, like Giulietta Masina or Edith Piaf next to bulky muscle men. The guard at the gate examined her pass, smiled, and let us in. I felt ridiculously out of place and nervous to be in a prison. Chantal was all efficiency and purpose.

"You here to cook the last supper!" the guard said.

"Uh huh."

"What's it gonna be tonight, honey?"

"New Zealand oysters, blackened tuna, truffled mashed potatoes, grilled wild mushrooms, Queen Mother cake with homemade ice creams and sorbets, and assorted petit fours. The wine list begins with a Veuve Cliquot Reserve Champagne, 1982; then Guenoc Chardonnay, followed by a Chateau Haut Brion

Bordeaux, and a Chateaux D'Yquem dessert wine. Port, cigars, and brandy."

The guard whistled. "I'd kill for that!"

"Well, *he* did!" Chantal shot back without a blink.

The prison kitchen was enormous. It echoed with a booming sound that had been made a long time ago, before we got there, before Chantal was born. Large cauldrons of steel hung side by side belling their toll sympathetically now and then. The cooks, huge men in white tee shirts, were cleaning up. The place reeked of the expected smells of institutional food vortexing together into a single odor—overcooked broccoli. One of the men, a prisoner, I guess, was swabbing the red-tiled floor with an oversized mop stinking of stale water. The mophead sloshed by our feet like a ropy medusa and then swilled its spoor onward, as we took soggy steps toward the stainless steel counters. I tiptoed my way through the effluvia while Chantal stepped directly with her Stairmaster legs and a steady eye cast ahead. One of the cooks recognized her.

"Hey Chantal! Waz hapnin', baby? You makin' Valdez last meal?"

"Yup, Darrel! You going to make it with me?"

"I'd like to make it with you!"

"Hey, you know what I mean. Cook it with me."

"No way, sistah. I gotta get home and feed my own. I'm not gonna waste my time spoon-feeding no rapist-child-murderer."

"Suit yourself."

"Hey, who your friend, Chantal?"

"Oh, he's a professor of mine."

"Watch out for him," Darrel leered at Chantal, "They pros, these professes. They sex crazy hangin' out with college babes. Know what I mean? Keep yo knife at yo side, sister! See you Pro-fess!"

Chantal smiled. She opened her cornucopic Zabar's bags and pulled out a neverending stream of provisions. I stood on the side watching her ministrations and feeling very much like someone who has always stood on the side and watched women cook.

Suddenly I was four, watching my mother chop liver, turning the dull-grey mass of crumbling meat into a paté by the deft, rocking motions of her half-moon cleaver. Then I was fourteen, watching my sister make brownies. I was the college boy watching my girlfriend make her special dish of macaroni and Velveeta with chopped bits of hot dog. Now I was the graduate student watching my lover make her trademark chocolate cake during the long afternoon her husband was out at work. But always, I was leaning against the doorway of the kitchen or lounging against the counter as women prepared food, a loitering Odysseus to some woman's Circe. It was all too familiar, though I cursed my fate for always being the one to watch.

Chantal was a miracle of efficiency. Aerobically she arranged the ingredients for the Queen Mother cake. She lined them up in the right order, and then I watched them disappear one by one into the institutional mixer like cartoon objects moving under the magic of a sorcerer. I wished I had that kind of art or that scope to cook efficiently. I had always enjoyed sitting back and watching, but now that was what I was contented least with. After she put the cake in the oven, she proceeded to the potatoes. She took their inchoate roughness and turned them into glistening ivory carvings, dropping them into the boiling water. Then she cooked the tuna, rolling it in Cajun spices and blackening it on an open flame, the scents rising up like burnt offerings on a hot day along the bayou.

She turned to me and smiled.

"Are you okay?"

"Just fine. Admiring your talent."

"Oh, there's not much to cooking. Like Wordsworth said about poetry—proper foods in proper places."

"I almost despise myself for not being able to cook like this."

She picked out some perfectly phallic mushrooms, took the tip of her apron and carefully stroked each ivory glans to clean it. Then she sliced the tip and stem with a Bacchic fury, creating neat cross sections. These she brushed with olive oil and sherry, placing them into a fiery grill to smoke their souls for eternity.

It made me happy to think of her. Her efficient castrations of the food were strangely comforting, and my state, like a lark at break of day arising from sullen earth, wanted to sing hymns, or at least Beatle songs, to her. I felt as if I was standing at heaven's gate with a dinner plate in hand.

"Does it bother you that he's a rapist, child molester, and murderer?" I asked, troubling the serene culinary waters with a pointed finger.

"Yes, how could it not?" She was scrubbing the gnarled, reticulated exterior of the oysters.

"And yet you are cooking for him."

"Yes." She said it like a child forced to confess to a misdeed. She slipped the knife into the oyster's side and slid it around, revealing the pearly, seminal interior.

"That's all? I'd expect you'd have more words than that."

"True." She paused and looked at me, knife in hand. "This is so complex." She slid the knife through the soul of another oyster, and said, "I think everyone should have a chance to eat really well in anticipation of death. Death transforms us. Valdez knows that this is his last night, his last chance to be in a moment, to savor something, to see the light, to feel the breath. That alone deserves something . . . a . . . sanctification."

"And you see this food as a sanctification."

"What else? I make it; he eats it; he must know." She was laying each glistening oyster in its scabrous shell on a bed of crushed ice.

"I guess he must." I thought she was right. I almost wanted to be the condemned man tonight. In fact I was. Someone once said that every life ends in an execution. It is only a question of when.

"Look, tonight he will eat this. It will be inside him as he walks to his death. Something of me will be within him. If I can affect him, this is the way."

Her eyes were opalescent. She offered me an oyster. We each held the bark-gnarled exterior in our hands.

"It's called Malaspina."

I put the shell to my mouth, but as I was about to let the cool slick of mucosal flesh slide down my throat, the evil-spined edge cut my lip. I looked at the oyster and saw a small pool of blood, vermillion against the pale membrane of the shellfish. I put the shell down and grabbed a napkin to blot my lip. Chantal looked at me and at the oyster with my blood. She picked up the shell, balanced its complex juices delicately, and then sucked the blood and the shellfish down her throat.

I did not know what to say. I thought of Christopher's blood I had been so fastidious to avoid. I thought of AIDS. I said nothing.

When she had opened the wines and laid out all the food on a cart, we watched the guards roll the feast down the somber hallway.

"Do you go to see him eat it?" I was still stunned by her impulsive act of communion with me.

"I did once, in another state, but I decided I did not want to."

"Why?"

"I think that is the condemned person's moment, not mine." She brushed a strand of hair out of her eyes with the back of her wet hand. "I felt like a voyeur."

I imagined myself seated in a cell eating this food and thinking about the dark woman who made it. Would I not want to eat her food . . . and then her?

"Have you ever . . ."

"What?"

"Given more than food."

She thought silently for a moment. Who knows what went though her mind. There was a trace of sauce on her finger, and she licked it. She smiled ruefully.

"The real question is am I rewarding horrendous crimes? Shouldn't the child rapist be tortured or plagued with pain before the moment of extinction? How can I, a woman, sanction an act of brutality?"

"How do you?"

"I do because we are all capable of it."

"It?"

"Murder, rape, mutilation . . . whatever."

"That's a cliche," I responded. "You and I may have brutal instincts, fantasies, but we are not going to commit crimes."

"We do it everyday, only we pay no attention. Every child who dies in Harlem, every kid who becomes a criminal. We permit it. By our inaction."

"Argument number fifty-three. I've been here before, and I don't buy it."

"Okay, so do you want to see Valdez's execution?"

"No."

"But you sanction it."

"Of course I don't. I'm against the death penalty."

"But what does that mean?"

"I didn't vote for Pataki."

"So you cast your vote, pulled a little lever, and you think your responsibility is over? What if Valdez was your son? Wouldn't you do more than pull a lever? Wouldn't you try to break into jail and get him out? Wouldn't you take heroic measures?"

"Yes, but I can't do that for every child molester who kills."

"Why not. Valdez is a person, and he's being killed tonight as coldly as you please."

"I don't please," I shot back.

"No, but if you hadn't come here with me you would not have known his life was going to be snuffed out."

"True."

"So why not see it happen?"

I agreed reluctantly. Chantal had the privilege, shall we call it, of witnessing the executions of the people for whom she cooked. Nowadays criminals no longer die by electrocution. That is too brutal, too obvious. Now the procedure is a medical one.

A guard brought us to a large, echoing room. We sat among spectators, varied people, who seemed to have nothing in common. We all might have been on the subway or in a doctor's waiting room.

Valdez was wheeled in on a gurney holding hands with the priest and mumbling Hail Marys. He looked half-drunk from his meal, and I could see small slivers of mushroom clinging to his moustache. He was a man of about fifty, darkly handsome. For some reason, he was wearing a Grateful Dead tee-shirt. He had already been heavily sedated. He looked at us and smiled, then he burped.

Chantal held my hand and whispered, "Prisoners in some other states can refuse the medical death. I heard of one in Colorado who wanted to be executed by firing squad. He wanted to make it difficult, uncomfortable for them. For the guys who have to pull the trigger."

Chantal spoke to me but she never broke her stare directed at him. He, in his sedated confusion honed into her eyes as if he knew something, as if the blackened tuna and the Veuve Clicquot imparted some special knowledge or at least directionality. She was right, I suppose, about the communion.

Two doctors came in with their faces concealed under surgical masks. One wore white and one wore blue. Chantal tightened her grip on my hand. Two IVs were inserted into his arms. The doctor began the drip on one. Valdez suddenly began to shiver, and then, without warning, in a monumental tremor, he vomited. All the food that Chantal had cooked welled up in his mouth, and he began to choke. I could see the bits of blackened tuna, the oysters in slick confusion, the slosh of the wines and the froth of the champagne. Everything she had worked to make beautiful and sacred was now reduced to a putrid swill. Valdez gasped, gulped, blubbered, as the room filled with the stink of vomit.

A small "Oh" came out from Chantal's mouth. It was a slowly descending sound, like hope walking down a hill.

The two doctors rushed around. It was almost too late, as Valdez turned blue, twisted in asphyxiated pain, and then appeared to die. But the doctors were not to be tricked out of their moment. The one in white pulled him up, performed the Heimlich maneuver. The one in blue had to perform a tracheotomy and intubate him. All the while, the press and the witnesses watched in various stages of horror. Blood flowed down the condemned man's neck, as the plastic tube was shoved with surgical precision into his trachea. A small whine came from his exposed larynx, which looked like large, white rubber bands.

Valdez's eyes opened in pain and horror. How strange for him to rise from the dead at this moment. As he saw the masked men, one in white and one in blue, did he think this was Hell? He began to flail around, breaking the IV's. Guards with expressionless faces held him.

"He's alive!" the doctor in white announced without irony. "Let's start the execution again."

Valdez tried to say his Hail Marys but only exhalations of gasping, tubular air came out of the tracheotomy. The doctor in blue inserted new IVs. I noticed that the doctor's hand trembled. One drip began, and Valdez appeared to fall asleep. Another one was turned on and in a tremor of rebellion and acceptance, he died. This time for good.

The limo dropped us at Central Park, and we walked all the way back to Morningside Heights. The night was colder than ever, and light snow was falling. I did not have much to say, and Chantal shivered a sob from time to time. The city knew, as it always does, that something had happened. Something always is happening, and so the city is forever reacting, only we, like animals who do not detect color, lack the perspective to see. The city is a huge organism of brick, pipes, wires, flesh, neurons in which organic and inorganic merge. It is immortal, eternal, and we are just the individual cells born and dying. But the city knows, as we know, of the transpiration of events. The buildings knew, and the street lights knew, and the slick of oil on the cobblestone knew. A life had ended brutally. The air was still, and night made grief seem stronger.

She invited me up to her place. It was as small as she had said and ornately austere. The whiteness of the walls dominated, but individual pieces of furniture, or fabric, drapery, made the apartment look theatrical. There were barely two rooms, and she could almost reach the door from her bed, just like Raskolnikov. The window gave onto what is grandly called "the courtyard" in New York; which means the airshaft, always dingy, cold, and ugly. I saw a man in another apartment sitting in his boxer shorts watching the cold, blue light of television. I could see the movie. It was *Rear Window*.

"I told you it was small," she said. "Is it what you imagined? How the other half lives?"

I looked around and noticed some men's clothing and shoes. Did she have a boyfriend? How could she not? I did not want to get into that old discussion about how bourgeois my lifestyle was, so I just smiled.

Chantal went into the bedroom to change from her cooking clothes, and I scanned her library. There were all the usual suspects—postmodernists, modernists, obscure French writers whose names always begin with B, the gangly array of Marxists, feminists standing with their hands in the pockets loitering next to the great old men of the nineteenth century—Marx, Freud, Nietzsche. Books on cultural studies all written by British men with the names Simon or Colin. Chantal stepped out rather spectacularly in a crimson sari trimmed in gold.

"What do you think of my books?" she asked.

"Many, eclectic, predictable to a certain extent."

"Predictable!" She did not like that word. "Here, look at these."

She directed my attention to a section of performance art. Each book depicted some bizarre alteration of the body. Men hammering nails into their scrotums; women having their mastectomies recorded; snuff performances; sex with animals; rituals involving bodily fluids.

"Okay, not so predictable," I gave in. "But from some point of view I might have expected you could have this. Who else would buy it? You are the target audience for these publications." I was still smarting from accusations of bourgeois lifestyle.

"Obviously, there is no escaping marketing," she conceded. "But then we are all *in* capitalism. It's just a question of *how* we are in it."

The night began to change and turn reptilian. The sky looked cracked and dry like the back of an iguana. Neon lights touched the clouds and marbled them with odd greens and iridescent scarlet bands.

I felt I should leave. I was married. I wanted my wife to return to me. I wanted my life to return to its dull routine. I did not want to argue about capitalism. I just wanted the image of Valdez dying in his own vomit to fade quickly from the klieg-lit theater of my mind. But the grief of the night, the sense of mortality, the desire for comfort made me stay.

"Don't you think that describing *how* you are in capitalism is just a defense mechanism?" I found myself unable to resist the lunge. "You justify consumerism because you like it. You like your clothes and your CD player."

"I'd give them up in second if there could be true equality."

I laughed. "If there was true equality you wouldn't have to give them up—everyone would have everything."

"That's only true equality of consumer goods." There was a pause neither of us could fill with words. "Let's change the subject." She, too, was getting tired of this tugging and pulling.

She selected some music. First we listened to some new recordings of Hündt's work. I tried to imagine faces in the music, but the only face I could see was hers. Chantal explained her theories again to me. Then she put on Schubert's "Death and the Maiden." I heard the strong opening bars, the maiden's pleading with death to let her live.

Chantal read the liner notes. "The maiden says, 'I am still young—pass me by,' but Death says, 'I am a friend, and do not come to punish—you will sleep sweetly in my arms.'" Chantal said, "You know I am very attached to death. I want to die."

"Now?"

"Why not? It is something I've wanted all my life."

"Not me. I want to live forever. Death is something I avoid like the plague." Why does the defense of life always sound so hokey against the nobility of nothingness, the existential appeal of the abyss?

"I dream of dying. I think of it as a pleasure, a desire."

"So, you will sleep sweetly in death's arms?"

She just smiled and made a small, humming voice as if she were agreeing with me, or with Death, or with Schubert.

"What about Valdez? Is he sleeping sweetly?"

"Now he is."

"It's hard to be romantic about death when you've seen a guy choke on his own vomit and then be resuscitated so he can be executed."

"I'm not romantic about death, I'm postmodernly existential. You'll think this is strange, but if I died tonight, I wouldn't mind . . . If you killed me, I wouldn't mind."

I looked at her complex, dark face and laughed.

"I'm serious," she said.

I felt strange, as if this would be the perfect end to a perfect evening. Execution followed by murder.

"How would I do it?"

She looked carefully down my body.

"Your belt," she said, and I felt she was speaking from experience not fantasy. "You could choke me to death."

"That's nasty. Your tongue would turn blue and you'd look just awful." I was trying to joke. "You've got what my mother used to call a vivid imagination."

"With your belt." I looked at her very thin and delicate neck. Schubert's quartet vibrated with rosin-whining gravitas.

Her long, thin fingers went to my waist and started to unbuckle my belt. I watched her take it off and put it around her neck, threading the tongue through the buckle. I started to say "Don't" but something else inside me took over. Something made me reach for the belt. I held it in my hand. She looked at me. There was a slight tension on the belt that encrimsoned a small almost imperceptible mark on her neck.

I knew I should not kiss her. I knew that I should not be here, but too many things had happened.

"Do you want me to kiss you?" I asked.

"If you do will you hate me after?"

"Why?"

"Because men do. The things they like in me before they hate after."

"What things?"

"Strong opinions. Irony. The fact that I don't fear, and they do."

I held my hand on the belt; I could hear the creak of the leather. I thought the belt was a bit ridiculous, but our lips touched. She kissed the cut on my lip, which stung as if sliced by the oyster shell again. Although I held her neck, it was she who led me into her bedroom. She was like a strong dog on a leash who gives its master the illusion of control.

How did I stop my hands from trembling as I brushed against the dark terrain of her body? At that moment, I could think of nothing but the jet stream that was swirling me, like the lovers in the *Inferno*, around and around my own desire, this lust in action.

Chantal was on her knees on damask-rose sheets. I could see the tattoo on her ankle again. It looked like two lions fighting, but I couldn't be sure. The walls of the small room virtually surrounded the bed as if we were inside a box. She touched my forehead with hot fingers that smelled of the food she had prepared—particularly the mushrooms and the black-spiced fish. I remembered that touch, that blind-fingered exploring-claiming touch. I hesitated, guiltily thinking of Anne. Fire fought with water; expense with waste; pride with shame. I felt suddenly filled with lies, death, blood, and blame. My donnish character, mild manners—were they really only cloaks for something savage, extreme, rude, cruel, and untrustworthy?

"What's the matter?" she said to me as I gazed at her.

"You look so beautiful. The most beautiful thing on earth right now." But I was lying, lost in my confusion.

I saw Valdez in his vomit. Death's scent curled through my nostrils. I thought if I touched her, I would never stop. I would become a criminal, a rapist. I would touch every woman I saw. I thought if I let myself go I would despise myself straight away.

Then something broke the stillness. How was it that her sari fell before my eyes like the unfurling of smoke? And how was it like rippling circles racing away from a stone dropped in a pond, sex began to undulate out from her and from me. Where the ripples met, there was an unsettling sea change. There she kissed me deeply, pulling my hand to her body. When I think of the moment, I think of the softness of her breasts, the point of her nipple; of the delicate skin between her legs; of wetness in our mouths and down our thighs. I was past reason. I bit her flesh as if swallowing bait. Her skin was like a poison that would drive the taker mad. I was the taker—hooked, trapped. Although I held the belt around her neck, it was I who choked.

No longer suspended, I was plunging into darkness. I was having her, but all the while I hated myself for passing any moment of reason.

We devoured each other like two of the condemned having their last suppers. Our tongues were on every part of our bodies. I could not tell which slickness was part of which body or where my body ended and hers began. Life had become one glistening strand of saliva against one straining stretch of flesh. The belt tightened around her neck, and she sucked on my painful lip as if she were nursing the last moments of her life. I almost thought it was possible to kill her now, to crown a moment of execution with a sacrifice of flesh.

I found myself on her back; she on the floor with her head against the rug. Madness swirled around us first in pursuit, then in possession. Her dark body was like the bottom of a sea. I gasped and tried to find the way to light. There was no light or air, only the thick confusion of arms, legs, hair, wine-dark gliding juice of the body. I came before I had a chance to enter her and felt myself losing the crest of excitement—had, having.

We waited in a kind of timeless dampness and then began again. I felt faint, failed. This time I was inside her. She had given me a condom. Her breath turned rhythmic. She moved quickly to her own pleasure, she cried out a name, a sound, something in one of her many languages that I had never learned, and then, after a long pause and quick breaths, there was the stillness of damask-rose sheets and the air heavy with humidity and bodies coiled in damaged heaps.

"Did you come?" she said with her open eyes, moving languorously.

"Yes," I said.

"Let me see."

"See? See what?"

"The condom. I don't believe you. I want to see."

"What?"

"You didn't come."

"Yes I did."

"Then let me see."

"I came before. Not inside you."

This insistence was awkward. The belt around her neck was loose now. Betrayal, the grim acquaintance, slid into bed with us. Making love had been a bliss in proof, even if my orgasm was premature, but now that I was no longer past reason, I began to find what I had done, with the pangs of guilt, a very woe. It was strange to think how what seemed before a joy proposed, now seemed like a dream. And it was increasingly becoming a bad dream. Her beautiful, dark body which had been dusted with an aura of desire, like dew on rose petals, was becoming increasingly mere flesh, with the defects, details, less-than-perfect parts starting to stand out like a photograph slowly coming into sharpness in a darkroom.

I could not help seeing Anne's body next to Chantal's. I was lying in bed with two women, each one reprimanding the other with their body types, their coloring. The fair one beside the dark one. I started to think about leaving. I began packing the suitcase of myself, gathering the toiletries of the mind, planning the route to escape.

How did I fail to know that little bit of commonplace logic that all the world well knows, but none knows well enough—to shun the heaven, the golden dapplings of desire, the sweetness of touch and kiss, that leads men to this hell.

"You don't like me," she said watching my receding self board the tramway to cold indifference.

"No, it's just that I'm nervous. The execution."

"You hate me. You think I'm a castrating bitch." She seemed to take some pleasure in that thought.

I liked her, but life was crashing around me like companion rocks. I had seconds to pass between them before they crushed me. Sirens were lurking on the shores; harpies picking at my intestines.

"I don't hate you." But I did. There was something extreme about her. How many women had wild schemes about Shakespeare, music, computers, cooked for the condemned, wanted their unknown lover to kill them? This was no simple liaison. No cheap date. One paid with one's life.

She looked at me through her darkly lidded eyes, and smiled. "Sorry to make trouble, but I need to know if people are being honest with me."

"Well I am," I said not being honest. "Did *you* come?"

"Yes."

I hated women for their bounty of pleasure.

"But it was . . ." Thousands of adjectives flashed before the screen of my brain, each with some detracting overtone. " . . . . ." I just trailed off.

"Unlike you to be at a loss for words," she said.

"Sorry. This has been a weird night. I liked you very much, but I have to go. It's not an insult to you. I'm just very confused."

I gathered my clothes and left like someone cast out of an alternative Eden. There were no words. The night ended with a whimper.

9

O, HOW I FAINT WHEN I OF YOU DO WRITE

"**S**hut the fuck up, you whoreson to a ratcatcher!"

Norman Goldman was in better spirits these days since he received the prestigious MacArthur grant that gave him five years free to do what he liked. Since he had been doing just that since he came to Columbia, the money was just gravy.

At present he was yelling at someone on the telephone, as I walked past his office. He now had a personal secretary to tend to his organizational needs. I tried to hide behind her as I slipped by the door, but he saw me and gestured to me with grotesque, voluble arcs of his arms.

"Will! Wait a minute! I've got to talk with you!"

He turned back to me and continued booming.

"Listen, I don't care if they offer me that kind of money! I'm not going to do it! I want double that! Who do they think I am, some unknown?" He turned and knowingly mimed to me in a "what-can-you-do" kind of way. I started to take a step out of his view, but he gestured even more ridiculously for me to stay, pumping his phone up and down as if he were pumping bilge water out of sinking ship.

He smashed the receiver down forcefully.

"Will, I've been trying to reach you. Can you do me a favour?"

I hated the proud, full sound of the "u" in that word when it came from his soft palate. There was a strong back-wind of karma and history behind Norman's casual requests.

"Norman, I'm in a bit of a . . ."

"No, I don't want to borrow something or live in your flat forever, Marlow. Don't fret. I'm a rich man now. I can buy anything I want. No, it's about Christopher."

Hearing that name caught me in the throat. There was some terrible violation about Christopher's name issuing from the profane lips of the Poet.

"Something wrong?"

"No, not exactly. You know he is a terrific fellow, compassionate, poetic, smart as a whip!" I wondered whether they *had* used whips—Norman possessed quite a collection of gadgets and Christopher had a penchant for slicing away at the body. "Anyway, he is at sixes and sevens. Doesn't know if he wants to act or go back to graduate school, write, or what."

"Yes," I said, feeling tongue-tied and a bit faint.

"Why don't you talk to the boy?" Norman suggested.

"I will, I will," I found myself saying eponymously. "I feel a bit inferior to you in this. You're so much better at making students feel comfortable."

Missing the jab, Norman smiled magnanimously.

"No, I'm sure you can do the job, even if your help is a bit shallow. Just keep him afloat, if you know what I mean. He rode upon my soundless deeps, but I think it might have been too much for him. He needs a quieter seas and a steadier bark to sail through on."

"Right Norman. I get the metaphor. How do I reach him?"

"Well, he's right here actually." Norman opened the door to his inner sanctum, and there was Christopher. It is hard for me even now to describe how he looked. I had to look twice because I thought, at first glance, he was a homeless man or someone severely ravaged by AIDS. Where was that American youth grown wild? He looked a medieval *memento mori.*

His long blond hair was shorter and rattier now, and it appeared as though it had not been washed in months. He was dressed in filthy jeans, and his shoes were like mud socks. Sores and pimples were scattered on his face. A blank expression glazed across his eyes. I could see the brown stains of old blood on his sleeves and cuffs where he had no doubt continued to lacerate himself. He brushed his hair from his eyes as his hands shook with a fine tremor.

"Norman!? What . . ."

"Oh nothing really, he just got strung out on some questionable medications. Why don't you take him home?"

"Home?!" I said *sotto voce.* "You want me to take him . . . home?"

"I thought you liked him."

I liked him. That was true. The simplicity of the statement struck. I took him home.

On the street, I was embarrassed. I felt, as if by association with his decay, I were rotting in the earth. I thought I would help him. This motive appealed to the best part of me. I would somehow make him over, find the immortal part of him and preserve that. Anne and the kids were still gone and would not be back for a week or so. A lot can be done in a week. He was mainly silent, except for bumming a cigarette from a passerby. He smoked in that bent over way of street people whose spines seem no longer able to carry the weight of their troubled thoughts.

When we arrived at my place, I suggested Christopher take a bath. He was too weak really to do anything properly so I found myself in the strange position of undressing him. Perhaps some part of me had wanted to see him naked, but this was not the way I imagined. His clothes were unspeakable, and I just let them fall into a disreputable pile on the floor. As they came off, tender, white skin appeared. Under his clothes he was not ravaged, just pale and thin, as if the elements did not have a chance to get to his inner body. His arms still had the *mille feuilles* scars and new fresh ones too. I put him in the pale blue water of the bath, slid him in really, and watched him. He was not self-conscious, obviously still high on something that made him nod out.

The water seeped into his pores and drew out the street dust. He began to freshen like a parched flower put into a vase. Layers of death and despair floated to the surface of the water and dispersed into a worldly scum around the edge of the bath. I let the water go out and filled it up again, as he trembled from the cold and the wet. This time the water around his body settled clear. I shampooed his hair and rinsed it out as I had done countless times for my children. Suddenly I missed them. My life seemed as though there were a crevice in it, as if everyone I knew had walked into the crevice and without being buried had morphed into nothingness. All I could hear was a fading echo of some primal utterance. I felt I had no one but this skeletal trace of a man.

"Christopher," I said in a whisper.

He looked at me as if he were not sure if I were a person or a wall speaking.

"Do you know who I am?"

He nodded. He knew.

"What happened to you?"

"I . . . then . . . " He shook his head as if chasing away flies.

I looked at him in his confused state. He was clean now. His hair slicked against his skull. He was still handsome, still preserved by the magic powers of youth which permit indiscretion without deep, tell-tale marks. His body was lean and his muscles defined in a flat, understated way as if nature had set him aside for articulation as a bas relief. There was something of a girl about him, and I had to glance down to his penis to remind myself he wasn't. It was floating in the water like a white anemone surrounded by the dark statement of pubic hair. It all seemed familiar to me. A body I knew and did not know. My own, my adolescent self, my son, my daughter. Like most men, I knew myself, caressed myself, was familiar with my maleness, but shunned it in another man. But here, in this moment, the passivity, the helplessness, the child-like neediness, allowed me to dwell for a moment longer on his sameness with me. And then the sameness did not feel alien, but like. I felt, for the first time in my life, that I could touch a man.

But I did not.

I had put him to bed, tucked him in as I did to my children. As I was hauling Christopher's clothing off to the garbage, a piece of paper fell out of his jeans. I unfolded it and read:

> That night of dark death
> as the sequenced turn took place
> as we rotated through the revolving door
> with its cool, metallic comment,
>
> we each in our own compartment,
> tied like bullets to a wall,
> culled like slivers from shards,
> barely acknowledged in my eyes that
> your eyes were disengaged
>
> gone like tree bark after leaf drop
> like the color of brick against the
> slick, blue steel of downtown
> like the tongue of sex and the
> taste of crack. How do I know
> your endless absent ways?

I read the poem and tried not to think about it. It was by Norman, no doubt. I sat down at my computer and tried to write my book. But I could not put a word down. Was it the proud full sail of his verse that made me hate Norman even more? The fact that it was bound for the prize of Christopher, who I suddenly found precious again, made my thoughts die in my brain. How could that crude, fat, boorish lout write this sleek stuff. Was it his spirit, by spirits taught to write, that struck me dead? No, it was the fact that he wrote about Christopher; that all I could do was write my academic essays; that he was, after all a Poet! And paid to be such. Did the academic powers-that-be care that he was a virtual pedophile, a sexual maniac? No. They paid him to be, to write about it. I could not praise Christopher and get a stipend for it.

Some hours passed. The phone rang.

"Hello."

"It's Anne."

"Anne . . ."

"What's happening, Will?"

"I'm not exactly . . ."

"Is *she* there?"

"No. Not at all."

"You've really done something bad, Will. You've done something damaging."

There was a long pause.

"Do you want me back?"

I wanted to say "Yes!" emphatically like a thirsty man who sees water, but I said,

"Do you want to come back?"

"We're married."

"I know."

"Are you sure she's not there. Are you alone?"

"No. Actually, Christopher is here. Remember him?"

"The boy with the cut?"

"Yes."

"What's he doing there?"

"He's sick. Wounded. Something. So I'm taking care of him."

"You take care of him? Why don't you take care of us?"

"I do . . . I did . . ." I said helplessly.

"Damn you to hell, Will. Why should I come back?"

I didn't have an answer. So I hung up.

I went to the kitchen and got a cup of coffee. I strolled through the apartment, but ended up at the door of the spare bedroom staring at Christopher in that way one stares at a distant body of land against a hazy stretch of sea.

10

SHE PRICK'D THEE OUT FOR WOMEN'S PLEASURES

My seminar went on the next day as if nothing had happened to me—as if Christopher were not lying in my spare bedroom, as if Chantal and I had not seen what we had seen, been where we had been. School schedules are ridiculously regular. Classes are always an arbitrary length of time. They begin and end with the stroke of an hour. Once, twice, or three times a week suddenly the same people appear at the same place as if by coincidence. And no matter what happens, short of nuclear war or catastrophic earthquake, the mirage of people appears again and again.

The mirage formed. Chantal was sitting in the middle of the class, as usual, wearing something black with silver lamé. Her eyes were closed, and even now I could not tell if she was bored, sleeping, or in a state of hyper-awareness. Did I have sex with her? Did a man die? I felt for the cut on my lip to make sure that something had really happened. The cut was there, something tangible. A fact.

"Sonnet 129" I found myself saying, "is Shakespeare's most obvious sonnet about sex. It seems to be about heterosexual not homosexual passion, though." Why did I say "though," I wondered as I talked on. "I would say that this is his sonnet about sex with a woman, specifically the dark lady. The poem comes right after 127 and 128, which introduce the dark lady, and right before 130, still about the dark lady. We have to assume that Shakespeare was not personally unfamiliar with heterosexuality since he was married and had children at this point. But somehow sex with this dark lady seems to him truly dark, infernal. He calls sex an 'expense' and a 'waste.' He sees it as 'murderous,' 'rude,' 'cruel,' 'a woe,' 'hell.' The question is—why?"

I looked around the room. No one answered. They all seemed wrapped in their own dark thoughts, or was it just morning languor?

"The sonnets about the young man are so full of love, admiration, devotion, but the ones to the dark lady are darker themselves. Sex is bloody and violent with her."

Gnostril's hand twined up.

"In the animal kingdom, sex is violent. Rape is the rule, so perhaps, in keeping with the work I've been doing on primates, Shakespeare saw sex with a woman as a kind of mating with the primitive . . . with the lemur-within, as it were, if you like."

"Thank you, Gnostril. I look forward to reading your paper on that subject."

A young man with an earring spoke up. "Professor Marlow, how do you know it was sex with a woman? Perhaps he finally had sex with the young man and it was kind of kinky . . . ah, sort of S and M?"

"Well, I don't know for sure. What do some others think?"

An African American woman raised her hand.

"I think this discussion is pointless. You argue over sex all the time—heterosexuality, homosexuality—but the issue here is her 'darkness.' What I'd like to know is if she is Moorish, that is African, like Othello? Could that then be the source of Shakespeare's discomfort? I mean you know how white men think about sex with black women? They think it's dirty. So does Shakespeare."

"Good point, Linette," I said. "I don't know if Shakespeare meant to refer to her as a Moor. Dark could simply mean dark-haired, dark-eyed as opposed to fair, which meant blonde. Actually the word 'blonde' or 'brunette' never appears in Shakespeare. The word 'blonde' spelled differently was used by Caxton in the fifteenth century, but the modern usage was reintroduced in the seventeenth century taken from the French. But if she was dark complexioned, there is a possibility she was foreign. A. L. Rowse thinks she is the daughter of an Italian music teacher. If that was the case, she might have Moorish blood in her, particularly if she was Southern Italian."

Linette looked disappointed at my pedantic answer. She probably thought I was just escaping from the Afrocentric issue. I was.

Chantal glanced with a look that claimed me. She did not raise her hand. She no longer had to.

"Oral sex," she said.

"Yes?" I could not tell if this was an answer or a request.

"It can't be about a man. It's about oral sex with a woman, cunnilingus."

"Oh I see. You think Shakespeare . . ."

" . . . yes, you see he clearly had oral sex with the dark lady and was both excited and disgusted. With the young man, he might engage in mutual masturbation and kissing—I don't think he was penetrated or did the penetrating. It must have been more like the ancient Greeks who engaged in intercrural sex."

"Inter . . ."

"Between the thighs, at least that's what Dover says. But here I think Shakespeare was compelled by the dark lady, obviously a very powerful woman, to go down on her. He calls sex a 'swallowed bait.' You see the orality of it? Now he never talks about this kind of orality when he writes about the young man. And Shakespeare 'despises' what he's done. If she had her period, then the 'bloody' makes sense. He is sucking, nursing really, on her bloody organ. Later in Sonnet 148 he describes himself as child crying after his mother, clearly asking to be nursed. Again this orality is associated with his relation to the dark lady."

I smiled. She was being clever, but there were no grounds to this other than perhaps her own desire.

"But where is the evidence? Most readings see this poem as about sexual intercourse, consummating the sexual act." I felt clinical and pedantic using those terms.

"Ah!" she smiled at me with a mix of superiority and flirtation. "Don't you see that the poem is not about consummation. It's about premature ejaculation."

"Yes," I tried to say neutrally.

"You see, with a man Will does not have this problem. He has his will. But with the woman he experiences the ejaculation at the beginning of the poem and it is a 'waste' of his semen. He loses his will when he becomes her Will. He is talking about how sex seems so powerful until the orgasm that tames it. Clearly, he had come during his act of oral sex but not in her. He does not satisfy his partner, this powerful woman."

I blushed internally, since I never blush externally. She was looking directly at my eyes.

"I see," I murmured stupidly.

"But there is more. I have taken the liberty of doing a computer search for the word 'tongue' in Shakespeare's entire work. Now, 'tongue' is a crucial word for him because it is both the metonymic symbol for poetry and verse, as when he says in *Two Gentlemen of Verona*, 'my tongue will tell the anger of my heart,' but it is also the actual organ. And guess what? Whenever it is the actual organ, it is often cunnilingus or analingus that Shakespeare writes about."

"Really!?" I was sort of astonished. I thought I knew this material.

"Yes, really. There's lots of references in *Taming of the Shrew*. You would figure in a play about a strong woman who has to be subdued this would be a big joke. So Petruchio says, 'Who knows not where a wasp does wear his sting? In his tail.' An obviously phallic reference, but Kate steals the phallus when she says 'In his tongue.' She claims the right to speak, but also empowers the tongue, thus letting Shakespeare turn his tongue, his writing, into a kind of sexual organ. Petruchio snaps right back, 'Whose tongue?' since he's trying to figure out if he or she is feminized by this castrating statement, and she says, 'Yours, if you talk of tales, and so farewell.' By saying that, she implies he is a chatterbox, hence a talkative woman, hence feminized. But Petruchio responds, 'What, with my tongue in your tail? Nay, come again, good Kate. I am a gentleman.' At that point she wallops him. You see, he makes it seem that she asks him to give her head, and then he demurs. Shakespeare makes the same joke again in . . . uh . . . *Two Gentlemen* when Panthino says, 'Where should I lose my tongue?' and Launce says, 'In thy tale.' To which Panthino replies, 'In thy tail!' So Shakespeare was clearly familiar with the practice of analingus and cunnilingus."

"An interesting theory," I said noncommitally.

"Well, and look at what Shakespeare had King Lear say about women's genitalia, remember? He says women are centaurs, above the waist belongs to the gods and below the devil? Remember when he says, 'There's hell, there's darkness, there is the sulphurous pit; burning, scalding, stench, consumption.' And in Sonnet 144, he just as much says that the dark lady's vagina is 'hell.' No, he wasn't neutral on the subject. He had been there and came back burned. A cunt was a hell-mouth for our little Will."

She let the four-letter words sink in. She was something to see, a kind of wonder. Her eyes flashed against the silver lamé. She was lithe, dark, intense, with a mouth that did not seem to stop making up theories. Did she believe this? Who knows? But she believed it at the moment. I was simultaneously embarrassed and astonished. What could I say? I said nothing.

In fact, no one said anything. The class had died and in the remaining moments I buried it. No one felt like challenging her, least of all did I. I felt blitzkrieged by this shopping-mall savant. She had dazzled me, fucked me, fucked me over, and now she was fucking up my class.

As I walked across the campus, I heard steps behind me. Of course, it was Chantal.

"I'm sorry. Did I go on too long? Did I . . . ?"

"Yes, you did." I didn't feel like thinking about her feelings.

"I know you thought I was talking about you . . . "

"Were you?"

"No, not really. It was a coincidence, or maybe not. Pos-sibly there are not coincidences only incidences which are all coin-ciding."

"Spare me your philosophy for today. I'm not feeling up for conversation."

"You hate me."

"Hate is too strong a word."

"You're angry?"

"Angry is too simple a word."

"Okay, so what is the weak, complicated word? 'Bored,' 'in-different,' 'annoyed'?"

"There is no word."

"Odd for you to say that. You ran out of words last . . . "

"Okay. Just leave it."

"See, I told you. Men hate me after. You're no different."

"I've got a problem at home."

"Your wife?"

I shook my head. We were at my apartment. "You might as well come up. I'll explain."

I made some espresso, and we talked. I told her about Chris-topher. I had never explained fully what had happened. As I was telling the story, she almost seemed to know what I was going to say. Her hands touched mine. She began her slow walk over my hands, reading them, moving on to my arms, and then again my face. I realized that she was hearing the music of Hündt's por-trait. I was telling her about Christopher, but she was registering other harmonics, building the fugue that was my face and neck, seeing sharps and flats along the contours of my being. I was angry at her. I was afraid of her, really. But as her fingers moved, I lost those feelings and suddenly I swirled into her.

And so, we were kissing like blind readers feeling the mean-ing of the words with our fingers and tongues. She had a way of forcing her tongue so deeply into the recesses of my mouth that she became part of it, as if she wanted me to devour her. Our teeth kept banging each other with a cranial thud as if the dull echo said we were really only two skulls trying to perform the impossible trick of making one skull fit into another. Sex with Anne had always been about two bodies touching and taking pleasure glancingly, but with Chantal I felt the aim was deeper, surgical, murderous in its intent to open the body up, find its darker regions, and eviscerate them.

Our clothes were off by now, thrown around, still clinging to arms and ankles. She grabbed my hair and edged my head down to her thighs. Her pelvis was arching, rocking, wanting my tongue in her tail, I thought for a brief second. Her eyes were closed, as they were in class most of the time.

I looked at Chantal's body. What Shakespeare had written was right. It was almost as if I could divide it into an upper and lower region. Above she was part of the angels, her pale amber breasts with their dark nipples, her slim stomach still damped with exertion, the arch of her hips, the vaulting of her rib cage, the architrave of her collarbone—all faced with the alluring dusky rose of her skin. But then beneath the waist, I only saw the hell mouth. There was another kind of darkness, the kind associated with the sulphurous pit. I saw with Dante's steamed eyes, the Renaissance vision of the devils standing at the open-ing with pitchforks and sadistic grins. I was the hapless mor-tal who had, for some now-forgotten, self-absolved sin in life, found himself naked and pronged with prods into my eternal punishment.

I put my tongue into the dark rising of hair, so strangely placed by nature in the field of the smoothest, softest skin, like a tangled and weedy pasture in Eden. Here things were knotty and gnarled, and my tongue tried to find sensitive, soft places pushing through the scratchy oblivion. Chantal moaned and reared her pubic bone. The complex smells of sex, blood, urine,

feces—the bouquet of perineal flavors like rich and strong cheeses—
swelled through my mouth and nose. I was disgusted. She was
right. And I was propelled at the same time by the quest of desire,
the ardor of the woman whose very core I was visiting, passing
through. I was pushing into Hell, devouring it, being devoured by
it. She was my Beatrice, my Virgil, my harpy. I was swooning in
the undulations, the swelling circles of her hips, the juices of her
moment, and she began to call in cadenced music somewhere
between a feral howl and a diva's aria. My thighs were wrapped
around her ankles. Intercrural, I thought for a brief second as my
body began to seethe with my orgasm and she voiced a last long
plaint, so that we came together and still separately.

I looked up at her face, my own wet and open with sex. She
looked down the length of her body at her leg marked with my
semen. Then she looked up at Christopher standing at the doorway watching us.

Christopher was back in bed, and Chantal had gone. I went
to see if Christopher was quiet. He was lying asleep on his stomach, a slight snore rising from his depths. The sheets had gathered around his ankles and his tee shirt had ridden up his back.
He was virtually naked, with the white cotton around his upper
back like the thin band around the upper torso of Michelangelo's
slave. Not that he was statuesque. He was rather thinner and
slighter, more like a Greek statue of a young man. The warm
light of late afternoon spilled across his pale flesh lending a
rosiness it lacked. The inner curve of his lower back yielded to
the rising of his buttocks and then a quick slope to his thighs.
I was standing at the bottom of the bed and my perspective was
foreshortened, offering more lower back than upper, more thigh
than shoulder. The effect of the angle and the light made my
vision painterly. He was relatively hairless, and as I looked at his
thighs, bathed in that light, I could see his natural beauty, that
which had been untouched by his life, by his hands. His buttocks were like a child's or like a young girl's, compact, creamy,
tinged with rose and light.

He rolled over in his unconsciousness. He had a woman's face, perhaps a woman's gentle heart, and when his eye opened for a minute it was brighter than a woman's. His penis lolled over his thigh, and the sight of it confused me. It was as if he were first created a woman, and then nature added something. I smiled to think that the very thing added defeated me. If my purpose was sexual it became nothing. He was pricked out for woman's pleasures, and if I wanted to love him, it would have to be triangulated through a woman's use of him. I thought of watching him as he had watched me.

As I said, I am not gay, and so I've never really been sure how a man makes love to a man. I can understand the kissing part, and the touching part, but the penis part is confusing, making an addition I do not understand how to use. Something about Christopher made me feel like taking care of him, kissing him, but what then?

"What, then?" I thought, and went back to the living room.

11

IN ME THOU SEE'ST THE TWILIGHT OF SUCH DAY

Then Christopher was feeling better. He was up and about. And he began to look better; like a man who has risen from the dead and is sitting down to his usual bowl of corn flakes. I began to realize that I barely knew this man who was living in my house, padding around in my sneakers. There had only been a casual conversation over a bloody wrist, a strange attraction. Nothing more. Yet somehow he had become part of my life and even more strangely he was becoming my life.

We were sitting down to breakfast. The corn flakes floated pointlessly in the milk.

"You know," I said, "I barely know you."

"There's not much to know." His fingers wandered to the scars on his wrist. "My family has a lot of money. My father was an inventor, and he built up a few businesses. My grandparents were Boston Brahmins. That's always given me a lot of freedom. It also makes me feel guilty, so I don't like people to know. I don't really even know much about my money. My uncle manages it, and I just get a check every month. It's not that much, but I can do what I want when most people can't."

I thought a little resentfully how I had to teach summer school to pay my bills. I folded my legs over my indignation like a man trying to keep an erection down.

"That's convenient," I said blandly.

"But I do try to make a difference. I live down on Avenue A. I do volunteer work with Habitat for Humanity, soup kitchens, things like that. Then I've been doing performance pieces at the Nuyorican Poet's Cafe."

"I thought you had to be Latino to do that."

"Well, they're letting in WASPs. It's sort of an unequal opportunity thing."

"What about your girlfriend?"

"What about her?"

"Well, are you still with her?"

"Sort of." He dropped the subject.

I was beginning to realize that conversation with Christopher was an exercise in frustration. He said things, but they didn't become larger things. One didn't seem to get anywhere. Yet, he was more than the sum of his words. It was not that he was inarticulate, but that his essential being did not take shape phonemically or semantically. Chantal was like a house of words on fire, but Christopher was more like a dilapidated hut from which emanated an eerie glow. There was another, perhaps stronger, force than words at work in the smithy of his soul, and this force could not be gotten at through banter.

When I looked at him, I felt the vector of his body, a light emanating with a Carravagio opalescence promising earthly beatitude. Christopher's blond hair, needing a cut, was becoming resilient again, picking up the glint of daylight; blood was finding its way back into his face. His youth, like a prodigal son, was crawling back on ragged knees to his strengthening body.

"The key thing for me," he said abruptly, "is the position of the moon, the stars, the planets."

Oh no! I thought. Astrology—perfect! That system of belief taken to heart by American naivete. The desire for deific bounty poured on our mundane lives.

"Astrology?" I inquired superciliously

"No, not astrology. I don't believe in that crap. I mean science."

"Science? In what sense?" I said, munching my corn flakes and feeling the annoyance of their crunch, their intrusion into my life. His intrusion into my life. Where were the long silent days of my research projects? The languorous days filled with quiet reading, solitary walks, and hermeneutic hours of lucubration?

"I'm obsessed really," he said obsessively. "Most people, despite what science they know, think they are living on a flat plane and that the sky is a dome above them." He formed his words carefully as if standing dominoes in a row.

"Yes . . . ," I said, not really having any idea what he was discussing.

"But that is not the case."

"No, it isn't," my interest flagging exponentially. I wished he would not talk. His voice had a measured, leaden quality to it as if it had never learned the ballet of humor that raises conversation from its knees.

"I try to keep in my mind at all times that I am standing on the surface of a globe. I am projecting out, perpendicularly, from the surface of this globe. My head is in constant contact with the universe."

I felt a sudden and overwhelming urge to water all my houseplants.

"So I have to figure out where I am in relation to the sun and the moon."

"What's the difficulty?" I was beginning to show exasperation in my voice. "Everyone knows that the earth rotates around the sun; the moon rotates around the earth."

"Revolves," he corrected me. "The earth rotates on its axis but revolves around the sun."

"Okay! Revolves! Fine! So, what's the difficulty?"

"The difficulty is trying to live that in real time and space."

"Is that difficult? I mean, don't we do that every second of our lives?" Whatever desire I had for Christopher was rapidly draining out of my body. How could I ever even conceive of an erotic connection with a man? He was wasting my time.

"Can you visualize a five-sided object?" he said somewhat abruptly.

"Sure," I said thinking of the Pentagon seen from the air.

"And a ten-sided one?" A building tried to come into view, but it blurred at its edges.

"Yes . . . well, no. Not really."

"Well, that's my point!"

"What's your point? I have no idea what you are talking about."

"You can say you know that the moon revolves around the earth and the earth rotates on its axis, but can you visualize where the moon is right now? Which way is it moving around you as you rotate on the surface of the earth."

"Not really."

"Yes, well! Then add the sun into the picture, and the planets. Can you imagine the rotations, the revolutions, as you stand on the surface of the earth?"

"No."

"You see, we stupidly think of the sun rising in the east and fading in the west. That isn't what really happens. You have to think of your body being whipped along the surface of the earth as the earth spins at 1037.5 miles per hour. Our bodies, speeding along really faster than the Concorde, make a complete trip of twenty-five thousand miles each day. But the earth isn't stationary. It is revolving around the sun at sixty-six thousand seven hundred miles per hour. And the solar system orbits around the center of the galaxy at four hundred ninety-two thousand one hundred twenty-six miles an hour. But even our galaxy is moving toward a point in the constellation Hercules at forty three thousand three hundred ninety-six miles an hour. Try to understand how those speeds fit together. And forget the sky. That's just an illusion. The blue sky is the same as the black night. There really is no sky, just sunlight messing up the constant vision of the blackness of the universe. And silence. There is absolute silence in space since there is no air to carry sound. Our heads are plunged into the eternal, endless darkness and silence of the universe, spinning at unbelievable speeds, with the moon, the earth, the sun, the planets whirling around in their own directions. And it's not a joke or an optical illusion. It's real. It's death's second self. And we just make it bland. Oh, look at the moon, dear! Isn't it beautiful? No, it isn't. It's a gigantic piece of rock hurtling around the earth, around our heads. Do you understand?"

I was trying to, but my mind could not fit into his compulsive, horrified vision of things. I thought his ramblings might have been the aftereffects of the drugs. There was an obsessive quality to his thinking that made me feel he was doing mentally to his consciousness what he had been doing physically to his wrist.

"Look," he said, and began arranging things on the table. "If the sun is this grapefruit, and the moon is this orange, and we are on earth, here is what is happening." He began to move things, desperately trying to understand his own position in all this citrus cosmology. There was a bereaved intensity in his face recognizable as madness, but attractive in that way that intensity draws us all into its orbit.

He's overtired, I thought.

I convinced him to lie down, and he promptly fell asleep like a child who has been overstimulated before bedtime.

The phone rang. It was Chantal.

"How is he?" she asked.

"He's getting better, but he has strange moments." I looked at him lying on the bed in a kind of golden innocence, and my heart went out to him. "He just got himself all worked up over the position of the planets."

"I know how he feels."

"You do?" I was surprised and suddenly threatened by her tone of voice.

"Yes, existential angst in the face of cosmic immensity. I feel it all the time."

"Sure, I do too," I lied trying to climb onto the intensity bandwagon. The truth was that astronomy, lived or otherwise, never kept me up at night. "You know, I realize it's almost impossible to really talk to Christopher. He's not into words like us."

"Oh, we just dress old words in new clothes, spending again what is already spent. But Chris . . . " I was surprised she called him "Chris." "But Chris . . . he's more than that. He's essence. He's the thing-in-itself. He's *Dasein*."

"Really?" Something was at war in me. I was drawn to Christopher by some unknown impulse, but now that I found myself near him, intimate with him, I had a need to make him loom smaller. Suddenly he was all faults, and I wanted Chantal to see them. But the effort to keep them apart suddenly felt too great, like trying to push against powerful magnets. She was young. He was young. I was older, lying on the ashes of youth like a man on his deathbed. I thought, let them have each other. So much did I attribute to her use of the contracted "Chris."

But I said, "*Dasein!* Don't you think you are over-Heidegerizing our young man?"

Chantal, with her invisible fingers probing every surface, ended it all in one simple jab. "Jealous?"

That is a question to which there is no answer and no denial, as Iago knew well. As Freud said, "Denial is affirmation." "No" just means "Yes," and "yes" only cedes power to the questioner. So I just dodged the whole issue and said, "I've been thinking of buying him a book, so he can write his thoughts down."

"A book?"

"You know, one of those handmade . . ."

"Sure, good idea."

Jealous. The word stuck. Was I jealous? Could I be jealous?

I dismissed the thought the way one dismisses a class. I wanted to see Chantal again, a craving rose in me to hold her dark, intense body against mine. I dismissed Christopher's body from my sensuous mind. He was a man. I was a man. My body did not crave that way. I cleaved to the woman. I wanted Chantal, her youth, her words.

"Can I see you?" I said.

"I'm a little busy."

"Oh, doing what?"

"Well, the Hündt stuff is taking up a lot of time now. I'm working with a very cool guy named David in the computer lab. I'll have something amazing to show you soon. And then there is another execution coming up, so I have do the shopping."

"Right."

"And to be honest, I feel you're not . . . into me, if you know what I mean."

"No. I thought I was . . . "

"Well, you don't really connect with me . . . physically, I mean. We're out of synch."

"But . . . didn't you?"

"Sure, I did. But you . . ."

"Well, you know, this is still new."

"I hate . . . " she said with lips that Love's own hand made, and I thought she was going to finish the sentence devastatingly.

"You hate . . . ?" I said languishing for her sake.

"Not you."

"Oh." Saved by the small efficiencies of syntax.

"I hate the institutional exigencies that force their way into our relationship."

I felt her slipping from me, shaking loose like a child who wants to go out and play. I was the adult inside the gloomy living room holding her back with a grip fashioned from the granite twins of habit and lack of imagination. She was invention, life, intensity, and I wanted to hold onto that since life had worn me down to my essentials—work, reading, my job. I was living inside the four walls of myself, and as she slipped from me,

I gasped at the claustrophobic reality of that tight, airless place. I thought, she that makes me sin awards me pain.

"You know, I've got my graduate work to finish, and you *are* my professor."

"Yes. Well, of course. But I never . . ."

"No, of course you didn't. But still you are . . . "

"Yes . . ."

"So, it makes it awkward."

"A bit, but only if you let it."

"Institutionally . . . "

"Yes, well, there is that . . . but . . ."

"Will, I need to think . . . "

"Sure, think, but don't . . ." I was going to say "leave me," but it sounded pathetic. "Don't hesitate to call . . . " That sounded worse, but it was too late. The words had made their entry onto the floodlit stage, and they had become players simply by the slightest effort of my breath.

"Of course not . . . "

She was gone. How can a moment of intensity become nothing so quickly? No doubt I would see her again, talk with her, perhaps even have sex with her, but she was gone. The affair was over, and all her fire and glory fled from me like a comet blazing away from this dull planet. I was cinders, burnt, cold, chilled for eternity.

Then I thought of Christopher and decided to buy his book for him.

12

THE VACANT LEAVES THY MIND'S IMPRINT WILL BEAR

"Norman," I found myself, against better judgment, asking, "where can I buy a good book . . . ?"

"What about my latest?" he advertised his glory with a flourish of his Armani-suited arm indicating a shelf blazing with copies of *Trysts Tropiques*. Norman's life-long slovenliness had given way to a new sartorial splendor. Since his attainment of the position of Great Man confirmed by his endowed chair and his MacArthur fellowship, he felt the need to dress the part. Norman's agent had suggested a public relations advisor who in turn suggested a personal trainer, clothing and color consultant, and speech coach. The effect of all these experts was to turn the boorish, messy, un-color-coordinated, slobbering Norman into a well-dressed, boorish, enunciating, color-coordinated Norman.

"And what about those covers? Will, this makes publishing history. The first book of poetry to be marketed as a best seller. See how they printed different covers in neon red, and that one in neon green with cut-outs? I'm going to outsell Rod McKuen, eh wot? Perhaps, even Stephen King."

"I hope so, Norman. But what I really want is a blank book. The kind you always carry around. Something special Christopher could write in."

"But he can't write a bloody word. He's illiterate, or might as well be. Why bother? Give him a coloring book."

"I think it might be therapeutic for him to write . . ."

"Blast your fucking 'therapeutic.' All you Yanks talk about all the frigging time is therapy. Face it, therapy is just a form of punishment—it's the iron maiden! You want to fit that boy into the covers of a book as if it were a straitjacket. You think everyone should write their paltry thoughts down as if every fool's gibberish mattered. As if writing calmed one down like chamomile tea."

"No, I just thought . . ."

"Will," he put his crushing arm around me with false avuncularity, "writing ain't Prozac! It's supposed to make you crazy, not sane. Look at me! Look at Mallarmé, Whitman . . . Blake! If they had had Prozac just think of the hollow there would be at the windy center of the world now. Do you see my point? Writing should give you a hard on, not heavy lids!"

"Yes, I do." I knew that with Norman one had to keep plowing ahead like a boat on rough seas disregarding the verbal swells. "But can you recommend a place where I can buy one of those books anyway?"

"Speaking of hard ons, Will. Are you screwing that boy?"

"What?"

"He's a lousy lay. Believe me," he said with his best leer. "I know. Get rid of him. He's bad business," he said, seeming to forget that he had just encouraged me to take Christopher.

That he was blamed by this monument to moral corruption should not be to Christopher's defect. Cankers like Norman love the sweetest buds. There was nothing for me to say. I turned and walked away.

"Schwimmers on Fifty-fourth Street," he called after me. "Tell them I sent you," he added magnanimously. "They'll treat you like a prince."

It took awhile to find the store, which was tucked between a large discount warehouse and an upscale restaurant. The place suggested an era that valued luxury, made deep and comfortable with dark mahogany cabinetry and shelves filled with leather-bound books. It was a store that rendered the customer immediately at ease with its excess while at the same time equally uncomfortable with the potential wallet-draining expense of everything in it. A salesperson appeared in a dark suit, speaking in sepulchral tones.

"I'm Mr. Sturbridge. May I be of assistance?"

"I'd like to buy a book," I said idiotically, immediately aware that nothing else was sold in this store.

"For what purpose?" He smiled in the way a lizard does before devouring a fly with a snap of the tongue.

"For writing . . . a blank book."

"Ah, for poetry, sonnets? That sort of thing?"

"Exactly," I said with relief.

"And would the book be for you?"

"No, for a friend."

"Yes, for a friend. Very good. And would she . . ."

"He, actually, he . . . " I found myself stuttering, betraying my secrets at the behest of grammar's insistence on the category of gender.

"Oh, yes, he . . . would he want something ornate or simple?"

It was a reasonable question. I tried to imagine Christopher with an ornate book or a simple one. I saw him sitting in an overstuffed armchair like some youthful version of Oscar Wilde writing in a book covered in filigree. Then I imagined him in black at a steel and glass table with an austere but elegant book. The fact is I really had no idea. There was something rococo about him, something about pages swirling with color. But then there was something Spartan about him in the sense of lined legal paper.

"Something between," I said.

"Exactly . . . the Aristotelian mean. We have some very nice books here." He handed me a selection of hand-bound, tooled books with vellum pages. They were wonderful objects evoking every English professor's linguistic wet dream. Their leaves were rich and creamy, the bindings sincere and devoted; the feel and the heft promised languid hours with a glass of port in one hand and a pen in the other. They were the transitional objects of adulthood, baby blankets in leather. I wanted to buy all of them and devote my life to filling them up with poignant ruminations.

"How much is this one?" I asked picking up an Italianate looking book that seemed to whisper *Nel mezzo del camin di nostra vita* to me.

"This one is one thousand five hundred dollars. Notice the *barzoletti* gold tooling. Very rare." Dante's rhyme slipped away from me like Francesca from Paolo.

"Surely." I covered my astonishment with the suave use of the adverbial form. "But do you have anything a bit more reasonable?"

"Yes, of course. However, you should be aware that our average book runs about nine hundred dollars. There is a lot of work, as you know, that goes into making these."

I wanted to walk out. Was I going to pay that much for a book and give it to a drugged-out guy with dirt under his fingernails who probably would never even use it? The impulse had been a nice one on my part. I am glad I had it, but I could pass on it now.

"By the way, how did you hear about our store?"

I did not want to say it, but the words sailed out effortlessly to fill the void of my embarrassment.

"Norman Goldman sent me."

"*Norman Goldman? Dr. Norman Goldman, the poet!?*" he said in italics.

"The same," I said with severe cognitive dissonance, observing the penumbra of respect playing over Mr. Sturbridge's pinched features.

"Well, then, you'll be wanting to buy books on the caliber of the ones he has purchased."

"That would be . . . ?"

"These!" he said pointing to a special shelf set aside under lock and key from the others. Here there were oversized, plumped up, dazzling creations. These were the Stradivarii of writing books, each of which proclaimed the uniqueness of the owner, the utterly special nature of the thoughts embraced between the lambskin covers. When he handed me one, the cover of the book yielded to my fingers like the velvet breast of a voluptuous muse whose sole goal was to make words flow out of the inner soul like seminal fluids drained from a hapless seducee.

"Beautiful," I murmured, immediately hating Norman for being able to afford these rare objects.

"Please, take one, for Dr. Goldman's sake."

"But how much are they?"

"Well, they are our most expensive items. That's true. But we can put them on account for you since you are a friend of . . ." he hesitated for a moment, " . . . the Poet."

I had no choice. I instinctively picked the most beautiful book I could find in quarto size. It was made of rag paper derived, Sturbridge told me, from the appropriated linens of Louis XIV, apparently stolen by a cagy footman. Practical artisans in the printing trade purchased those upscale rags to make the kind of paper they'd only dreamed of. The cover was of Persian lambskin decorated by a renowned Hapsburg atelier. The book had been a present from a noblewoman to Voltaire, and he apparently was planning to write *Candide* in it. When he was forced into exile, he unwittingly left the book behind. It was completely empty except for a "V" in the upper left hand corner of the first page which had been identified, Sturbridge confided, by experts as the initial autographic consonant of the *philosophe* himself.

A haze of confusion clouded my eyes as I left the store. New York seemed to be shrouded in smoke though which pedestrians slowly strove with determined, somnambulistic expressions. Sturbridge waved goodbye, mumbling about how some unspecified amount had been entered on my new account at the store and how the book would be delivered by armored guard to my home within forty-eight hours. Later I was not entirely surprised to learn, when I received in the mail a crisply folded bill from Schwimmers, that I had somehow spent $8,500 plus tax on this little *cadeau* for Christopher.

The armored car did indeed arrive bearing its gift. The door-man called up and told me that someone with a gun had a package for me. For a second I thought it might have been one of Christopher's old drug pushers. When I went downstairs, a Wells Fargo officer accompanied by another guard, hand on holster, glancing from side to side nervously, gave me the book boxed, wrapped, and bubble-packed from Schwimmers. As I walked upstairs to my apartment, I felt like Moses carrying the tablets of the Ten Commandments, only in the wrong direction.

Christoper was at the dining room table working on a papier mâché model of the solar system.

"I've got something for you."

He looked up distractedly as if he had forgotten some vital detail of his own identity.

"A present."

"What is it?"

"A blank book. Fill up its vacant leaves with your mind's imprint."

"Yeah, good idea." He grabbed it and absently put it on the table. Small globs of papier mâché flour paste clung to the Per-sian lamb cover.

I grabbed the book back, only managing to rub the glue further into the binding. "It's kind of expensive. Take care of it."

"Really, how much does something like this cost?"

I was a bit flustered. I couldn't bring myself to tell him how much I paid.

"Oh, not too much." I dodged the question, cheapening my gift in both our sights. "But you can make it worth more by writing in it."

He took the book back, and now feeling justified by virtue of its seeming cheapness, laid it down again amidst the wet papier mâché strips.

"I will," he said as his eye wandered back to the soggy universe he was constructing.

I thought, "To take is not to give."

13

MAD SLANDERERS BY MAD EARS BELIEVED BE

So I found myself in the middle of my life's road in some obscure forest of existence. My wife had left me; my dark mistress had closed her legs to my desires; my young, platonic friend had come to live with me; and my life took on a desultory, unfocused quality that made me feel as if I were half alive. I began to wonder about the parallel universe I was constructing in my own life and how it seemed to mime that of Shakespeare's. But the miming was off a beat, out of synch, as if the mimer were drunk or deluded. Do things in life happen randomly or do we set up the conditions for their arrival? Was I building my own house or simply living in one made by another?

My course on the Sonnets was caught in the quagmire of my personal life. I could barely drag myself into class, and once there I had nothing to say. Chantal stopped attending. Gnostril sank deeper into the Borneo rain forests of himself. The feminist, the African American, the Marxist, even the Jesuit began to leave the course like audience members exiting a bad play. The quietest students, sensing the power vacuum left by the absence of argument or opinion, became emboldened and started to talk more, creeping out from their rodent nests of dullardry to feast on the cheese of conversation. Consequently, the table went bare pretty quickly. Inane comments piled up on vacuous observations until there was nothing left to say. We simply began to read the sonnets out loud. We were up to Sonnet 78. When each sonnet was finished, everyone would look around and nod. A few people would exhale loudly through pursed lips or murmur inarticulate expostulations under their breath. Then the next sonnet would be read. Criticism and analysis winnowed down to gusts of air, grunts of assent, or low-drawn whistles of admiration.

I felt responsible, but I was too depressed to do anything about this twice-weekly ritual of empty appreciation. Soon the grunts and nods began to disappear and the class was no more than an endless recitation unpunctuated by even the pause that would break one sonnet from the other. Life had become Art, and Art had become lifeless.

I began forgetting to attend class. The first day was a shock. I resolved not to miss class again. But then when I missed the second class, it became easier to forget the third. After a few weeks, I barely sensed anything was amiss. My presence didn't matter. The reading went on, and when the class finished with the last sonnet, 154, it began again, like the endless cycle of reading the Torah. The class had become a perpetual recitation machine no longer needing me as the academic clock maker or *primum mobile*. Reading aloud became a kind of mantra, and the class a ritual prayer session. Education, the process of leading someone somewhere, as the Latin root *educare* suggests, had become a closed circle. The class did not need any leading and like a brainless ox went around in circles tethered to the post of poetry. Occasionally, I would peer in from the hallway and see the students sitting in their infernal circle reading the poems aloud. I passed by the door unnoticed, unnecessary.

It was not too long before I got a memo from Samuel Morse, the eminent Victorian chair of the department. He wanted to see me. He had sent a terse note about our needing to discuss some things.

"Will," he said smiling and stepping forward to greet me with a vigorous handshake that is the hypocrite's prelude to inevitable bad news.

"Will, I understand that your class on Shakespeare is not in tip-top form."

I made no effort at defense and simply shrugged my shoulders.

"Will, there's a rumor that you are no longer attending your own course. That can't be the case, can it?"

"Well, I wouldn't put it that way, Sam." I used his first name back to him as if hitting the corporate tennis ball back into his court. "You see, the students are really doing some intensive group work now, and I believe it's better that they are not overly influenced by my opinions or even presence. You know those experiments . . . the ones that show an observer can change the results of an experiment. It's really an amazing paradox, since how can you conduct an experiment without an obs . . . ?"

"Will," he cut me off. "How are things at home?"

"Fine, Sam. And you?"

"Fine, but I've heard that you and your wife . . ."

"Anne! Oh Anne's visiting her parents. They are getting older, infirm, and need her help. It's nothing really."

"I've heard that you are living with a . . . former student? A male . . . ?"

"Oh, ha! That's really funny. The rumors. They really get it wrong. I'm not living with . . . that former student. Not at all. I'm just helping him back on his feet. He's had some bad luck and . . ."

"Will," he cut me off, again. "Have you seen the letter?"

"The letter? No. What letter?"

"You might want to read this. One of our doctoral candidates, a Ms. Mukarjee, wrote it as a kind of public communication. She's sent copies to all the students and faculty as well as to the school newspaper, the deans, the provost, and the president."

"Oh," I said with the quarter ounce of air allotted to my lungs as I began my near-death experience.

Morse handed me a ten-page, two-sided, single-spaced epistle that I hastily grabbed and put into my jacket pocket.

"You know, Will, far be it from me to interfere. But this is Columbia. Students expect a decent education. Their parents pay for it. Alumni rest their careers on it. Wealthy donors have their names carved in stone for it. I don't think the reputation of the English Department will be enhanced if these people think that students are being abandoned by their professor."

"Sam, it's not abandonment. That's putting it a little strongly. It's independent study."

"Will, if you need some help. Some counseling or a rest . . ."

"No, I'm fine. Don't worry. Things will be back to normal in a jiffy." I found a bracing comfort in the colloquial ending.

I shook his hand and left clutching the letter. On the way out, I passed by my class, who happened to be meeting at the moment. There were only about seven or eight students sitting in a circle. Only now instead of reading Shakespeare, they were reading Chantal's letter aloud. I slouched by.

Ten pages single-spaced. Damn her loquaciousness! I stumbled out between the Doric columns of the building and collapsed on the cold steps of Low Library like a piece of flotsam on a marmoreal sea. It was a bright spring day and hundreds of people were perching there trying to store as much sunlight as possible in their spiritual solar collectors.

I squinted at the pages before me, whose dense, single-spaced typing looked like some tract written by an insane propagandist intent on proving the existence of God by paranoiac algorithms. I read:

> Dear Professor:
>
> I am writing in this public venue, the locus of print and the public sphere, so that the transactions that occurred between us will not be confined to the putatively private space of your office or home. These bourgeois boundaries, deftly constructed by hundreds of years of patriarchal, oligarchic consolidation of power, both through primitive accumulation of capital as well as rigidly defined parameters of ideologically enforced bio-power, with such devastating results to women, blacks, the disabled, the trans-

gendered, third-world peoples, and so on, are the institutional trappings of power that disguise the actual economic relations of people to people, what Marx called "the real relations" in life.

I do not intend to embarrass or humiliate you, and for that reason, I will not use your name. But I do think that the events that transpired between us are in fact part both of the educational and institutional process which in its largest sense is transactional and public. For that reason, I will not hesitate to describe things that would normally be called private or belong to what has been called the domestic sphere. The history of privacy leads us to understand the civilizing process, as Norbert Elias calls it, as a consolidation of bourgeois and patriarchal power. For that reason, it would be a mistake to allow the private to cloak questionable activities insofar as they have public consequences. And here let me add that I have no aim of harming or hurting you but only of improving the educational process under which we, as un-unionized graduate students, labor.

The relations between professors and students, especially ones between male professors and female students, but by no means excluding gay, lesbian, bisexual, transsexual, and transgendered have in the past been considered private affairs (I use that word with all its resonances), but since the passage of anti-discriminatory legislation (liberal at best and enacted only at the provocation of the now-spent, middle-class, mainly First World, feminist movement) such relations have been redefined as having relevance to public life.

To begin the elucidation of power politics not only within the English Department and the University, but in society at large, I will undertake to place in narrative, to narrativize, a set of personal transactions between myself and you.

I first met you, Professor, at a musical concert in which I was a performer. Without any provocation, you approached me and began to discuss inappropriately various aspects of my physical appearance, including details of my personal anatomy. You commented on my body and asked me if I worked out. You were accompanied by another professor in the department who made rude and sexually explicit comments when he thought I could not overhear them. I immediately critiqued the gendered nature of your comments, but you basically ignored my remarks.

Professor, although you may have thought our encounter was a private flirtation, you obviously were unable to see that power relations were operative from the first. Your position in the professional-managerial class gave you the economic stability from which to launch your assault, although you would no doubt not call it that. I, as a graduate student from a multi-cultural background, also under the sway of your institutional power, since you might in the future be ruling on my promotion and certification, was clearly in a subaltern position. The metropolitan discourse that informs your behavior was also a factor in the postcolonial relation established between us, with regard to my meridional subject position determined by my gender, racialized color, colonial status, economic position, and so on. You seem to have been blithely oblivious to these obvious factors determining our interaction. In fact, throughout our transactions a kind of "haunting" occurred in which power and patriarchy became a ghostly *revenant* of bad faith.

I had already pre-enrolled in your sonnet course when these events transpired, so I hardly felt it appropriate to drop out, especially since it has not been unknown for professors to take reprisals in other venues such as accreditation, recommendations for teaching assistantships, and so on. (I know you would not do this, but on an institutional level one is never sure.) When I arrived in the course, I was first surprised by your lengthy discussions of sexual matters and your obsessive dwelling on the sexual context of these works. While I agree with you and many other theorists that the body is clearly a central focus of all literature, especially erotic literatures, I do take issue with an under-theorized relation to the body as such. As Judith Butler points out, the body "itself" is itself a myth made to foster artificial gender divisions. There is no body, per se, but those social, political, and economic relations justified in a Foucauldean sense, by established power. So, to describe in detail and orient the class toward the body in a rather crude and untheorized sense is to participate in the larger politics of oppression. Your approach particularly, shaped by your own unacknowledged subject position as bourgeois, white, middle-class, heterosexual man, who, though you espouse a left to left-liberal position, masks a deeply conservative if not regressive political orientation.

I say this, Professor, with all due respect to your personal motives. I have no doubt that you are a "good" person under some personal strain in your home life. (I make no judgment on adulterous behavior since I do not acknowledge the bourgeois contract relation known as "marriage." I do however see adulterous behavior combined with matrimonial regulation of women's bodies as another form of patriarchal oppression. Finally, I agree with Nietzsche's notion that a married philosopher is a comic figure.)

I also have no doubt that you seek progressive political change as I do. However, your approach to such change, an approach that emphasizes personal good will, individual acts of kindness, and some general notions of enlightenment ideology (the fairness of the democratic process, the worth of individual thought and artistic creativity, a blindness toward the pain of unequal distribution of wealth) leads you ultimately down the wrong path away from liberation and toward oppression.

To continue my narrative, you frequented my work place, and when I came to see you at your home to ask you to help me in a research project, a research session turned into a sexually charged encounter. You then told your wife that I was the cause of the misunderstanding that ensued when she discovered us together, which precipitated her departure. When you found out about my work with prisoners, you expressed a strong wish for me to take you first to Sing Sing, and finally to my apartment where we had a sexual encounter. While I have no wish to describe that encounter in detail, I do have to add that your sexual modus operandi is one that leaves no room for female *jouissance*. Your use of sadomasochistic techniques, while certainly a free choice for any consenting partner or partners, combined with your tendency toward premature ejaculation, while no doubt a painful thing for you to deal with in your personal life, is worthy of public comment insofar as both participate in a history of patriarchal oppression of women. Premature ejaculation, along with priapism and other types of sexual variation (I avoid the word "dysfunction"—seeing it as part of an oppressive medicalization and policing of the body) are not simply biological mechanisms but contain a heavy weight of cultural content, being as they are somatic semiological statements of contempt for the female body and for female anatomy. (It is interesting how much you stress Shakespeare's repulsion toward the female body in your class, by the way.) Domination and bond-age, while a necessary choice in any free-thinking couple's sexual repertoire, can also contain an overdetermined signification, par-ticularly where unequal power relations obtain—as in the case of professor and student. While it is true that technically my life was not in immediate danger as a result of your practices, I do think that experimenting with strangulation on a partner who might be at some physical risk (someone with some latent spinal damage, hyper- or hypo-thyroidism, and so on) could present a major health-related risk. And while I doubt you are actually capable of homi-cide, it is worth noting that you did discuss the possibility of my being murdered by you as a possible outcome of our relationship.

Further encounters between us were characterized by this continual restatement (*repetition*) of your power both as a man and as a professor in the form of an active oppression of female *jouissance* through premature seminal emissions. (The symbolism of your ejaculating on my thigh needs little interpretative comment at this point, although there is a very interesting essay to be written on male fetishism of female loins, from Zeus' enwombing of Dionysus in his thigh to D. H. Lawrence's overuse of the word and his fear of female orgasm.)

I want to add immediately that the scenarios I have described were not of the date-rape variety. I consented to the sexual inves-tigations on both of our parts. There was no personal compulsion, and so I would be more than reluctant to bring sexual harassment charges against you. Indeed, it is my deep belief that such use of the law is really a regressive step since many of the suppositions behind notions of financial restitution to the "victim" and depri-vation of liberty or financial fines as punishment for the offender are deeply capitalist and bourgeois in nature. Professor, I would never claim that I was an unwitting female victim or dupe of your Svengali-like powers of seduction. Far from it. However, having said that, I do feel that every moment of our sexual researches were imbricated with the inequalities of power that are inherent in our institutional relationship. One cannot escape this "haunt-ing" by the *revenant* of past violence made abject under patriarchy which returns like the repressed in everyday encounters. These are the micro-threads and tendrils of power that my open testimony here is meant to elucidate and, of course, combat. Let me state again. I am not seeking redress, vindication, or punishment. I am seeking clarity, openness, and a way of using our encounter as means of education, in the largest sense of the word.

The letter went on for another five pages. It detailed some more of my relations with Chantal, mentioned some things about Christopher, and generally left little to the imagination. It ended with the following:

Dear Professor, I hope you understand my motives, but even if you don't, my purpose will have been accomplished.

Yours in struggle,
Chantal S. T. Mukarjee

When I rose to my unsteady legs after reading the letter, I was another person. I felt like Oedipus, Job, King Lear, Jude, and the entire Kennedy family compressed into one tragic figure. Blood dripped down my sightless sockets; sores and boils covered my body; I held my dead daughter in my arms and beheld the unjust justice of life as the blood of assassinated family members pooled at my feet. And through all, I had one thought. How could she do this to me? Hadn't I been courteous? Hadn't I asked her permission along the way? Didn't she seem to be excited by me and our relationship? What about my connection with her Hündt project? Did this make sense?

As I walked back to my apartment, I thought of Christopher. He seemed the only thing of value left to me, like a loved one who had survived a devastating airplane crash. Was this personal blitzkrieg of my life worth it to me if I somehow was left only with him? Why did I even like him? He was mostly silent, except for the endless articulation of his personal relation to the cosmos. He was living off me and taking advantage of me far more directly than did Norman and Delilah. Yet there was a something noble, still, and quiet that radiated out from him as if from a worthy graven image. His self-mutilations, his pain, his drugs were all a protest against his more solid self which abided like the Catholic Church or the pyramids.

The apartment was now beginning to look like the solar system itself. Various papier mâché orbs and satellites were hanging from chandeliers and door frames. Christopher even began to motorize some of the objects so that they were starting to rotate and revolve. The technology was very simple, since he was fashioning motors from my kids' toys and our household gadgets, but the inanimate universe was coming to life, as if given motion by some not so unseen prime mover. God was not a cataclysmic force but a strung-out tinkerer; creation was an obsessive hobby.

Christopher was hard at work and barely noticed me when I entered in my distraught state. His arms were beginning to take the toll of his increasing stress and for the first time I began to realize that he was cutting himself again. Dried blood clung to his wrist as a reminder that all was not well.

"Hi," I said.

He looked up.

"It really makes a difference," he said, "whether the things we live with come from above or below the ground."

"Have you read this letter from Chantal?" I asked without following his line of, or lack of, reasoning.

He shook his head negatively and continued. "Like all the plastics and metal . . . all from below. Gas, oil, petroleum, kerosene, polyester, naugahyde, Formica . . . all that stuff is from below the earth. On the other hand, cotton, wood, linen, wool, plant and animal dyes, our food . . . all that comes from above the ground." He looked at me for some sign of agreement.

"Look, Chris, a terrible thing has happened to me, and it involves you."

He looked concerned, briefly. But the overwhelming logic of his argument carried him along like a paper cup on white water rapids.

"You see, Will, this all came to me on an airplane. I was sitting there trying to figure out which direction we were going and how the rotation of the earth fed into our own movement. Does a plane go faster or slower if it is flying in the direction of the earth's rotation? Anyway, I was feeling uncomfortable, nervous, and I suddenly realized that everything on the plane . . . everything . . . was made of stuff that came from below the ground. If there had been wood and cotton, things like that, can you imagine how much more at ease we would be? If planes ran on firewood, wouldn't you feel more comfortable?"

"Probably . . . but Chris . . . this letter."

I looked into his obsessed eyes and suddenly I had no desire to tell him about any of this. Why should I burden him with this? His fault is youth, after all. Better to keep silent than speak. This is nothing, and nothing will come of nothing. I'll hold my tears.

Shakespeare's words echoed around me like Job's comforters. I had taught the Bard so long that his thoughts had become mine. Were they bromides or solutions? Or were they just words? Was I more sinned against than sinning? Could the world be more weary, flat, stale, and profitable than it was now? A tear ran down my cheek, and this Christopher saw, perhaps because it was an aboveground phenomenon. He put his arm on my shoulder, without a word, and my armored self clattered onto him. At that moment, his body seemed the only strong, upright, and resilient thing on this earth capable of keeping me from falling in a disordered heap on the floor.

This was the first moment we really touched. And what struck me was the abiding strength in him. I had really only held women in my life, their bodies generally smaller than mine, their arms—even with the assistance of the Nautilus machine—less bulky and protective. Here was a quiet, inhering power. The power to do hurt, perhaps, but the restraint to do none. There was something stone-like, granite about this strength, slow to temptation, unmoved and cold like the judicious beat of a heart.

I put my arms around him, and felt his flat chest like a wall, not inwardly yielding the way breasts feel, but permanent, unwavering. His hand stroked my head and suddenly I was the child. Where was my father? Long dead and moldering in a grave on Long Island. No one had fathered me for years, and just now I wanted a father to fix the broken strands of my life. I wanted someone else's strength since mine had gone.

Did he pick me up, or did I imagine that? I felt lifted by an exterior strength, something without a name or even a face. It was a force that lived now in me, now in him, now in another. Something we passed around us when the need for power was in the air. Sometimes we give it to kings, or presidents, or parents, and so I gave it to Christopher.

It was not as if there was a decision to kiss each other, but rather kisses enveloped us, and so we became part of that decision. The feeling of roughness next to smoothness was what struck me as the odd thing about kissing a man. His lips were soft and beautiful, but I could feel the scratchiness of his upper lip and cheeks. This too reminded me of being kissed by my father, the kind of kiss a kid wipes away with the back of his hand. I had a desire to push him away, to push the heat away that was arising between us. Somewhere it felt wrong, unfamiliar, like sweetness in a meal when the palate expected salt. I heard the word "homosexual" in my ear, whispered by some conservative think tank of the mind, but I could brush that away like an annoying fly. After all, this is the postmodern age.

Our breaths were taken faster, and our hands began to move with familiarity. I felt his hardness through his pants with a strange recognition. There was sameness, not difference.

But it was different for me, used as I was to sliding along the regularly smooth contour of a woman's body. The old knowledge of my fingers trained to find the inside of things was foiled by the exteriority of his passion. The outrageous obviousness of male desire was almost too demanding, too much lacking in subtlety. Woman's arousal is a hidden thing, with tell-tale traces discovered by detective fingers, lubrications that slyly bespeak themselves, but this was bold speaking, flailing insistence. It was the thing-in-itself. It could not be disguised.

Christopher peeled off my pants with an experienced hand, while I fumbled about for his zipper. Without a word, he was upon me, that strength translating itself into action decisively. His mouth was around my penis, and I fell back in a virtual faint. I had never had a man do this to me, and of course it was not so different from a woman, with one exception. He knew exactly what he was doing. He wasn't making love to an alien organ, the flesh of another, he was giving pleasure to his own. He knew the inflection and the slant of my desire as if he owned it.

When he lay on me, I could feel his penis nosing its way toward some unspecified goal. It felt suddenly like a near- sighted mole pushing and pushing its way to its own pleasure. So this is what I was like, what all men were like—hairless, blind rodents bent on shoving their insistence against whatever flesh or into whatever hole or crevice they could find. But then it was also the glory of the phallic–Doric columns, proud uprightness, erect heads, powerful rockets hissing heavenward. His phallus was between my thighs. Intercrural, I thought, just as Christopher ejaculated onto me. His semen matted into my leg hairs and wet the floor beneath me so that I felt as if I had peed. I felt his energy wane, and thought about Chantal. I understood.

But we kept kissing, as I remained in the position I had no doubt put Chantal, and my desire began to grow as his failed. I wasn't really sure what to do, but Christopher turned over. I was lying on his back, so smooth and creamy, like a woman's. It was the same foreshortened image I had seen that day when he was asleep in bed. His buttocks and back were like polished ivory. He looked like an idol from some lost Greek cult. His hand reached around, wet with his saliva, and guided me. How, I have no idea, but I was inside him. I thought immediately of AIDS, but I had no will any more. I began to move slowly at first then with speed. I cared no more about my life, my family, my career. All that mattered was this moment. I never felt more connected to the physical in my entire life, and yet never did I feel more virtuous and honorable. It was as if sex had become a platonic thing; it had become pure sex without gain or hope. I came inside him with a crashing silence, like a wave on a looming rock. I was never happier in my life.

14

LET NOT MY LOVE BE CALL'D IDOLATRY

It is not that I loved Christopher for who he was; it was that I loved him for who he wasn't. That was the definition, I realized, of platonic love. He wasn't perfection, but there was something in him, in that silent place at his center, that suggested the way. He was like the earth, like life, flawed and imperfect, but fair, kind, and true. Christopher was a door through a lower mystery to a higher one. He was the physical portal through which I had to pass to get to the universals. So, I had become a platonist simply by lying on my back, or on his.

My immediate reaction was fear that I had become a homosexual, that I was no longer what I had known myself to be. I also worried that I had contracted AIDS, hepatitis, or a sexually communicable disease.

"Have you been tested?" I managed to ask him.

"A year ago. I was clean."

"But since then?"

"No. Have you?"

"Me? I've been married."

"Oh, don't let that fool you. Maybe your wife has been unfaithful. I know you've slept around."

"Not really. Only with Chantal."

"Well, she's been around."

"True." I thought I should get tested immediately and so should Christopher. But the thought was so embarrassing. Should we go together? What if someone I knew saw me? I resolved to make sure I had condoms around in the future.

Christopher said, "How did you feel about fooling around with me?"

"Fine," I said, muting all my doubts to a syllable. "Great, really."

"You know," he said, "that I'm not into men on the whole."

"Me neither," I said, thinking of Norman.

"But a man can do to me what a woman can't."

"Oh," I said like an ingenue.

"There's nothing like that feeling of being . . . "

"Sure, I can imagine." I imagined Norman ramming his poetics up Christopher's implied reader.

"Have you ever . . . "

"No, never."

"But . . . "

"Do you mean have I ever been . . . " I tried to find the word. " . . . penetrated?" It sounded so awful and clinical.

He laughed. "A woman can do a lot, but she can't do that."

"What about with a . . ."

"Oh, come on, it's not the same. Latex versus warm flesh."

"What does it feel like?" I asked.

"It's like being two men. Male in the front and male inside. You really get in touch with your masculinity, with masculinity. You know?"

"Uh huh," I said, but really didn't know and didn't particularly want to find out, especially if masculinity meant a small, blind, insistent rodent burrowing into my intestines. "I had too many bad experiences with enemas when I was a kid. My mother was a great believer in them and suppositories."

"Well, if you ever . . ."

"Sure, but things were fine the way they went," I said quickly.

Christopher's eyes floated over to the papier mâché solar system, and I could see that our conversation was almost over. Then he turned back for a minute.

"What was that you said about a letter?"

"This," I said showing him the *j'accuse* document.

"I'll read it," he said.

My name had been branded, and I wanted his pity. I felt in some way that his pity could cure me. This vulgar scandal was stamped on my brow like the mark of Cain. I didn't care what anyone else thought of me—well or ill. Christopher had become somehow my all-the-world, and his shame or praise was what was important.

A few days passed. There were nights and days. The days and nights began to merge. He never mentioned what he thought of the letter. We did nothing but stay at home. Our provisions were running low, but I could not bring myself to go outside. I didn't want to be seen by anyone, such was my humiliation. But also, I had developed a child-like fear of separating. I wanted to stay with Christopher. Our days had cycles that revolved around sex. I don't think I ever had so much sex in my life. With two men, there's more sex. I can barely remember the specifics of what transpired, although I maintained my injunction forbidding entrance from below. But we did things that tested the letter, if not the spirit, of that law. In all, time became a body, and our bodies were lost in time. So he became dear to me. He had become my sweet boy.

We were lying in bed. The sheets swirled around us reflecting the strong light of approaching summer. Our bodies were cut out akimbo, arms and legs, a rudeness of elegance dappled with titanium white, solarized. We were a study for some ambitious painter with a Renaissance vision and a nineteenth-century temperament.

Christopher said, "About that thing of Chantal's?" His voice rose up in that familiar way.

"Yes, what did you think."

"Well, it is awful. But it's nothing. Nothing unusual, just that she put it into words. She has a way of doing things like that."

"Ah, yes, but she did put it into print. And print has a duration. Life is short; art long."

"Don't worry. It will be all right."

He touched me protectively, and we started kissing. Our naked bodies seemed to glow with inner light transforming the coarseness of male flesh into something finely wrought. Pure geometric forms—circles, rhombuses, trapezoids—rotated into three dimensions as we twisted our contraposto bodies and gyred into each other.

That was when I heard the key turn in the door, and familiar voices scampered in. They were small and roving. My children, followed by their mother. Anne's timing was impeccable. A simple message was burned into their retinas. I was naked and in bed with a man. I had only moments to see the horror on all the faces. This moment was colossally worse than when they found Chantal's fingers on my face. Anne was not even able to pull out a "Gosh!" or a "Heavens!" The kids gazed with the fixed stare of Russian icons. Anne blanched, took one step back, and fell wounded to the floor like someone assassinated.

Do I have to tell the details of my leaping out of bed, tumescent genitals bouncing and flailing with each staccato movement, Christopher rising up nude and gleaming like an alabaster column in the agora? The children scattered as if they were small game diving into a thicket. Anne was a corpse. We carried her to a couch and slapped her a bit. She began to rouse. When she was back in her wits, she looked directly at me, now wrapped in a sheet like a poor imitation of Socrates.

"You!" she said, using the monosyllabic pronoun as combined summary and judgment of all my crimes.

"Anne . . . " I trailed off into some nether world where apology was unnecessary, replaced simply by eternities of sadistic, punitive torture.

"What *is* this?"

"It's . . . love."

"Love!!?? For who?" She never got the proper use of "who" and "whom" down, despite her patrician upbringing, but I felt it would be wrong to correct her at this moment.

"I'm in love . . . with Christopher."

"Really! Well, let me not to the marriage of true minds admit impediments!"

I smiled wanly. I guess all my Shakespeare had filtered down to her, finally.

"The only person you love, Will," she added, "is yourself."

"Anne . . . "

"Don't . . . " she shook her head. "So, you're gay? Has that been the problem with us?"

"I'm not gay. I'm . . ." I couldn't think of the word.

"You're a fuck. That's what you are. What, are you bisexual? Who do you think you are? Shakespeare with his young man?

"No, not that. I'm not anything. I'm just doing this now. Here. That's all. Does it have to have a name?"

"It doesn't have to have a name, but it has a face," she said, glaring at Christopher who was trying to amuse the kids with his solar system.

"I know. Sorry." I added pathetically.

She looked almost as if she understood. Then a shiver of hate rippled over her, and she closed herself to me, I felt, forever. She got herself up, tore the kids away from the small universe of Christopher, and left.

15

'TIS BETTER TO BE VILE THAN VILE ESTEEM'D

The divorce materials arrived by courier in due time. Calumny began to be heaped upon me. I rarely ventured out of my bower of bliss, but when I did I inevitably ran into two kinds of people—the shunners and the inquirers. A number of my colleagues were shunners who seemed not to see me on Broadway, and their pointed avoidance expressed their thoughts. The inquirers were worse, as when Betty Johnson, a colleague in anthropology, stopped me at the Food Emporium.

"Will, how *are* you?" she asked over the melons.

"Okay, and you?"

"I'm fine, but I hear that you and Anne . . . "

"Yes, well, it just wasn't working."

"It's for the best, isn't it?"

"Yes, I've got to go . . . " I said, edging toward the peppers and the exit.

"So, what was it?"

"Just drifting apart."

"But I heard, I mean there are rumors, that you . . . "

"Oh, don't believe everything you hear."

"So, you're not . . . "

"Not at all."

"Well, that's terrific!" And she sailed off not a bit fooled by my subterfuge, as I contemplated some moldering shiitake mushrooms.

The worst, of course, would have to have been Norman. I managed to avoid him for a while, but I did have to go into my office. Like a predator patiently waiting for the prey, Norman was poised. I heard a knock on my door, and I decided to ignore it. Suddenly I heard the lock open. Norman appeared all smiles.

"I've gotten your key from the sec'y." He said the abbreviation with an ironic flourish. "I wanted to make sure your plants were watered." I looked over at my black, withered philodendron. "Sorry, old man, but I could have sworn my amanuensis had done the job. By the way, your clothes really need some color coordination. See my colorist. Blue looks hideous on you."

"What are you up to, Norman?"

"Rather, the point is what are *you* up to?" But before I could say a word, he continued, "Did you hear? I'm up for a Nobel Prize. Seems like *Trysts Tropiques* has garnered some praise in Europe." He sighed like a man weary with flattery.

"It's a good book. Not that good. But if they want to give me the bloody Nobel Prize, why should I stop them?"

"Why, indeed?" I sank a little lower into my unendowed chair, hoping he would unload the dump truck of his ego at another location.

"Will, what about that letter? She's a devil-bitch that girl. What spunk, eh?"

"Norman, I'd rather . . ."

"When I see her now, after this, I tell you Will, I want to swive her so fucking hard that she'd see the *aurora borealis* on the ceiling."

"She'd only write about it, Norman."

"Not faster than I would." There was no beating him to the rhetorical punch these days.

"What are people saying about me?" I asked tentatively, realizing that I was asking the executioner to tell me if I had any color in my cheeks.

"Well, there's good news and bad news. The bad news is: they say you're finished. Your class is a scandal. This letter is a major embarrassment to the department and the university. I hear, by the way old chap, that the *New York Times* is going to do a story on sexual harassment here. Looks like you'll be the poster boy. And, of course, the thing about the wife leaving and the rogering of young Christopher doesn't sit well with the *éminences grises* here. The alumni and donors don't like this moral turpitude. Of course, damn if I care, but that's the way it is among these hypocrites."

"What's the good news?"

"The good news is that I'm screwing Hillary Clinton. Don't tell anyone, because I've got the Secret Service crawling all over me. I met her at a cocktail party in my honor. She's a fan of the arts, and we hit it off. I guess it's a kind of revenge over the Monica thing."

"You're kidding me."

"Would I kid you, my dear boy? And I'll tell you. She's hot. I mean really hot. There's something about the reins of power. That woman makes love like there's no tomorrow. Why did Bill ever want head from Monica? I have no idea."

Was Norman fucking Hillary Clinton? Anything was possible. I didn't really care if he was in bed with the Virgin Mary.

"Norman, what am I going to do?" How did it come to this? I was asking my worse enemy for advice. And I meant it.

"Well, Will, I'd say you're in a pickle. Get rid of the boy. That's the first step."

"But I . . . " Was I going to open my heart to this egomaniacal swine? " . . . love him." I gave in like a bedraggled and bloodied rooster in a cockfight.

"Hmmm. You love that little nonentity, do you? What is there to love? He's hopeless. He can't tie his own shoes. Will,

he's living off you. He tried it with me, but I booted him out."
Norman obviously forgot that he booted him out into my naive
arms. "And he can't fuck worth a horse's turd. He's a loser. Deep-
six the rotter."

So much for love.

"Oh, by the way, Will, why not come to my investiture in
the American Academy of Letters. Next Sunday. And how did
you like that book from Schwimmers? Nice stuff, eh? I bought
myself a few more. Although somewhat pricey? Good thing I've
got a research fund to cover my expenses."

Strangely, my visit with Norman was the best part of my day.

The door to my office shivered with a knock. It was still ajar
thanks to Norman's prying key. One of my students from the
sonnet course poked her head in. Her name was Jennifer (so
many of them were).

"Can I talk with you a moment?"

"You may," I corrected without her realizing it.

"I just wanted to let you know that the course . . ." I was
cringing. " . . . was one of the best I've ever had."

"It was?"

"Yes. I really like the way you gave us the freedom to express
ourselves. So many other professors would have dominated the
course, but you took a back seat."

"Well, actually, I tried to . . ."

"That was what was so great. This is the first time in my
graduate career that I dared to take an active role in the course.
When you released control of the course, so many of the . . .well,
more vocal . . . students left. That was when I found my voice."

"And what voice did you find."

"Well, it was just my own voice. This one." This one was
reedy and squeaky, underlarded with a thick cushion of phlegm
and restrained by the invisible ballast of labored thinking. "I felt
fully realized for the first time in my life. Thank you."

"You're welcome." I wanted to kiss her hem and cry in her
lap, this being the only act of kindness I had received from the

outside world. It made me think how little students ask of us, that even our absence is a bounty to them.

"And about that letter from that girl in our class?"

"Yes," I said cringing again.

"I thought she was rude."

"Oh, did you?"

"Yes, if you did that stuff with her, like she said you did, well, that was private. Even if you did do it." She batted her eyelashes at me, and I suddenly realized that she had come to flirt with me. Clearly Chantal's letter had the unintentional effect of acting as an aphrodisiac to this reader. I was now the fast boy in the school. The telltale signs were there. She had dressed up, put on makeup, and was leaning forward in her chair revealing the decent cleavage that God had given her to elicit a response in men the way that a happy face decal elicits smiles in infants. Was I one of them?

Then I had a paranoid thought. Suppose she was a stringer for the *New York Times?* The more I thought about it the more I decided she was clearly on assignment. No one could be so stupid as to think that a professor's abdication of teaching responsibilities could ever be glorified as a pedagogical innovation. How could I bite at this preposterous lure? I tore my eyes from the lactational *gestalt.*

"I'm busy now," I said coldly. And then blurted out, "Tell that to the *Times.*" She looked completely confused, as I ushered her out of my office cursing the media, spies, and bitches who write public letters.

I turned to see the dark shadow of Chantal waiting in the hallway. I gasped inwardly. She, of course, looked amazing— dark, beautiful, strangely dressed in a short skirt with pants underneath and a leotard top. She had cut her hair and spiked it blue. The look was definitely pugnacious if not pugilistic.

"Don't be angry," she said quickly.

"Why not? You've broken confidences. I'm in incredible trouble now. What happened to your sense of truth and justice?"

"I still have it. That's why I wrote the letter."

"You wrote the letter because you wanted revenge. You're jealous about . . . him."

She gave me an impossible look and said, "How could I be jealous about him when I broke up with you before that?"

"People are complex."

"Will, you've got to separate the personal and the political. Personally, I am very fond of you. I will always honor our moments together. But institutionally . . ."

"Okay, I got that. I read the letter fully . . . several times."

"Oh, Will, I knew you'd take it the wrong way."

"The *wrong* way! What is the right way?"

"You know, with a little distance. Like the way Che Guevara might have listened to Fidel making a critique . . ."

"And how did you become such a Marxist?"

"I'm not. I'm beyond Marxism, but I think that we need to incorporate elements of a Marxist critique into a feminist, deconstructive matrix."

I looked at her. She was a piece of work. A wondrous shoal devised by Fate for me on whose alluring rocks I was destined to wreck my ship. Her pretty looks have been my enemies. It was almost worth it—the pain, the humiliation, the suffering—almost, but not quite.

"Chantal. You destroyed my life . . ."

"Will. I didn't destroy your life. You were a free agent acting in accord with your own wishes, insofar as anyone in late capitalism can." She paused. "But that's not why I came. I don't want to rehash all this. I said it as well as I could in my letter."

"So why did you come?"

"To invite you to see the Hündt project in completion."

"The Hündt . . . "

"Yes, you remember. I've been working with this guy in the computer lab with the latest technologies, and we've accomplished something really amazing."

"You're having sex with him." It seemed clear to me that Chantal eroticized everything and everyone.

"Oh, Will, that's not what I'm talking about."

"But you are having sex with him."

"Yes," she admitted. "But that's hardly the point."

"Hardly."

"No, the point is that the project is done. I'm thrilled, and I really want you to come and see it since I used your face to crack the code."

"More than the code."

"Oh, Will. Just say you will."

I paused. She looked at me like a kid asking for a trip to Disneyland.

"I will."

"Great! You won't believe it."

She kissed me on the cheek and left in dazzling vortex of energy and perfume.

"I will." I echoed my plaint through the empty hallway. A cry to pure being seeking to strive and not to yield.

16

THOU ART ALL MY ART

I managed to pull Christopher from his stationary orbit around the jerry-built orrery long enough to attend the unveiling of the Hündt project. He put on his decent clothes, a pair of black leather pants and his denim jean jacket. We walked over to the computer lab, where we met on the way Norman, Gnostril, as well as some of the other students from the sonnet course. They all had looks ranging from hostile to uncomprehending on their faces when they saw us heading to Chantal's grand opening. I knew they had read the letter and were trying to figure out how this premature-ejaculating, sexist-dominator had the nerve to further impose himself on this unfortunate graduate student in her moment of glory.

We entered the computer building and found our way through a fluorescent labyrinth of illuminated dullness into a room without windows filled with computer equipment. Chantal was there dressed in a man's black tuxedo which she had draped multiculturally with a black and red Indian shawl. With her was a generic-looking graduate student who was obviously the computer whiz.

"Will," she said, "I'm so glad you could come. You, too, Chris. This is Dave."

Dave adjusted his oval, wire-framed glasses, scratched his goatee, and shook my hand. He seemed like a fine young man. I hated him instantly for wending his fiber optics into the body, if not soul, of my dark lady. It took a few minutes for all of us to settle down, but in Norman's case this was a near impossibility. He was posing, posturing, and leering at everything under thirty-five. Eventually, Chantal stood up and cleared her throat.

"Thanks for coming," she said in the American-as-apple-pie voice that belied the intelligence of her comments. "As you know, this project is one that I've been working on for several years. It's been kind of a personal quest for me, not only in terms of my interests, but in a way a journey through time to the past. If you haven't heard me talk about this by now, I've been trying to crack the musical code of the composer Hündt's work. He wrote musical portraits of people in the late Renaissance, and my theory has been that these portraits were not simply impressionistic but real representations. I have finally finished my project. And what I have done is to transcribe the musical notation into digital information that can be made visual in the form of three-dimensional computer images."

Christopher nudged me and whispered, "That's what I've been doing with the solar system. She and I, we both want to realize information in three dimensions . . . even four if I add the space-time continuum."

I smiled wanly. I felt that everyone was smarter than me, working on incredible, if futile, projects that tested the limits of being human, whereas I had accomplished nothing. I had written three middling books, taught trivia, lost a wife and children, and gained only this young man to my left whose half-life of affection for me could only last several weeks more if I was faintly lucky.

Chantal ran her fingers through her blue hair, shot a pointed glance at me, or was it Christopher, and continued.

"With the assistance of David Tannenbaum, who is doing his doctoral dissertation on consistencies in random access systems, I have at last been able to realize in visual terms the abstract musical notation I have puzzled over for years. There are many people here I want to thank personally, but my special thanks goes to Professor Marlow, without whom I could have never deciphered my Rosetta Stone—the musical portrait of the Earl of Leicester."

She smiled at me, and meager scattered applause crackled through the audience. I looked around and Norman nodded approvingly, while Jennifer, the graduate student I had unceremoniously booted out of my office, sat stonily. Gnostril, who in the ensuing months had grown a beard and really was now actually starting to resemble a lemur, appeared to be picking nits off his arm. The rest of the graduate students and faculty stared in confusion, no doubt remembering the anonymous letter.

"So, without further discourse," said Chantal, "let's see the result." Special glasses were distributed, and we all put them on. The lights were darkened while Dave began to operate his equipment. A projector kicked on with a hum, a few beeps and coughs issued from the computers, and then in the center of the room an image began to form. It was life-sized; a man, but unfocused. Along with the image we could hear what sounded like somewhat drunken, if not deranged, Renaissance music. The image became clearer as Dave adjusted some knobs. It was a three-dimensional image of . . . me.

"You may recognize Professor Marlow here. In order to understand Hündt's Earl of Leicester, I had to first make a template of finger-locations on a subject who resembled the Earl. In my research, I realized that Professor Marlow was quite close to the visual representation of Leicester. If you look at the slides behind the image, you will notice the similarity." She flashed a slide of the Earl and one of me walking on Broadway, which she had clearly taken with a telephoto lens unbeknownst to me.

"You can see the similarity. When I gridded Professor Marlow's face in three dimensions, using Hündt's finger-notation, I could then transfer that information to the musical portrait of Leicester, although I was off by some sharps and flats. And this is what that piece looks like."

Then, as she played the musical tape of Hündt's original work, a being began to form in the void. The feeling was uncanny, as if one were present at the opening of a pharaoh's tomb. The past began to unfurl like a butterfly emerging from its chrysalis. As the music proceeded, transforming from sound to digital recording then to light beams in microseconds, the figure began to be constructed before our eyes. We saw first the top of the head, his dark hair came into view, a long forehead, feminine eyebrows, a long, thin nose, a pointed beard, ruffled collar, and then the image stopped, suspended in midair like a levitating, living bust. The music continued, and the head and shoulders moved, smiled, and said something. I could almost read its lips. I thought he said, "Good my liege," but it might have been "Would I leave?"

"I haven't been too successful in generating anything below the shoulders in this piece. I'm still working on that."

She walked over to the image, attempted to put her arm around the Earl's shoulders. The fit almost worked, although the obvious insubstantiality of the projection next to substantiality of Chantal's biceps was apparent. Nevertheless, there did seem to be a chumminess between the image and the woman, especially as she chucked his chin. The audience laughed nervously at this quasi-miscegenation of historical incontemporaneities.

Chantal invited us to walk around the Earl. I stepped over, face-to-face with the very person I had seen only in woodcuts and oil paintings. I communed with the Earl for awhile, but he seemed to stare right through me at someone else. I wondered who.

As I turned to go back to my place, I saw Christopher and Chantal eye-to-eye in conversation. I noticed a familiarity I had not seen before. I heard a harmonic of pain in the music. The two of them were like embodiments of my comfort and my despair. If the man is an angel, I thought, is the woman a devil?

Norman grabbed at my sleeve.

"Amazing! Will, do you realize that with this invention the past can be recovered. We don't need Proust anymore. Just think, old man, people will be able to know what I was like in three dimensions thousands of years from now. That vixen's got to do my portrait. Full body, of course," he added leering. "She does this by running her fingers over the flesh, eh? She'll have to go the length and breadth of me. Maybe I'll have her do Hillary, too."

His desire for visual immortality was intoxicating. The moment of living in someone's retina forever went like energized photons through Norman's id to his ego without the usual check-in at the toll house of his superego. Norman in two dimensions alone was enough to give me pause.

Norman said, "Next to this, words are nothing. Shakespeare was a dope when he said that his young man would live immortally through words. Proust was just hot air. What are words, Will? Something barely more than farts issuing from the lips, right? But Hündt! He cheated death. Shakespeare didn't come close, the poor rotter! Ah, but Hündt would have been nothing without the vixen! And now she can do for me what Shakespeare thought he was doing for that young punk. You see, we have absolutely no idea what his young punk looked like, Will. Shakespeare forgot to tell us that." Norman was inebriated with the possibility of being remembered in his corpulent effrontery forever.

Chantal, too, was exhilarated with her success. It was truly an accomplishment. And Dave seemed in his modest, computer-nerd way to be enjoying the moment. Norman began besieging Chantal for his birthright of immortality, offering her increasingly large amounts of money, fame, and rapturous sexual favors. I couldn't tell if Chantal was biting.

After a time people began to leave. I tried to drag Christopher away from Chantal, but that was more difficult than bumping him out of Jupiter's orbit. Both to each seemed to be a friend, or more so.

Chantal turned to me and said, "Will, please stay. You, too, Chris. I want to show you both something."

After everyone had gone, Chantal whispered, "I didn't reveal all. There is something else I need to keep secret."

I wondered what that could be since she didn't keep much secret.

"Dave," she said with a certain authority, and Dave jumped into action like a well-trained spaniel. The music began again, this time with a special jig-like quality. "It's a complex piece of music. First it is a jig, then a branle, then a gavotte. Fitting that it should be so complex."

"Whose portrait is this?" I asked.

"Well, it's . . . Shakespeare's."

"What!"

"Yes."

"But I didn't know that Hündt ever met . . . "

"Well, that is the crowning piece of my work. It seems that in 1698 Hündt had taken a trip to London. This is when he wrote his "Arcadia Anglia," a long vocal piece, a kind of auditory tour of England. A section called "Thespis on Thames" was broken up into several smaller passages and given titles. The one that caught my attention was called "London's Fair Loves and London Lovers Fair." In it I found a long aria with the lyrics, "There is much a' do about nothing when love's labours are lost." When I applied the grid to those musical phrases, I saw a face I knew. Unmistakable. And here it is."

The computers clicked again, and the musical theme began, sounding much like what I had always imagined the songs in Shakespeare's plays to be. In a matter of seconds, like a genie out of a bottle, Shakespeare was before us. It was the face we had seen in the National Gallery portrait of him, the one most of us know. But it was different because it was alive. No longer the stiffly wooden man, there before us was the living one. He breathed, blinked, and was both more and less handsome than he had been rendered. This was no bust, but the complete man. He was well dressed, elegant in his movements, and yet had a kind of nervous, pent-up energy that made him look edgy and ill at ease. When he walked, he did so with a limp. He appeared to be lame and somewhat bent over.

No one could talk. We just stood in a circle around him, if I can call a representation of Shakespeare to be the man. In fact, the distinction between representation and being seemed to drop away as it does in a good photograph or painting. Some solemnity and sense of ritual made us take each other's hands, in a way to try to enclose what we were unable to grasp. Shakespeare said something to someone. He spoke a few sentences. We strained to read his lips. It seemed as if he said, "To those who love in vain, sing to me of the vanity of love; to those whose love is doomed, dirges we bring to the tomb." But he could have easily said, "Do those whose luck in pain sing to me the inanity of the two; to those who love two, we bring the dew." My eyes strained to understand him, to receive this message he was sending the posterity he had so desperately sought to reach. But he might have been saying anything. He was a kind of Delphic Oracle, some text available for many interpretations, yet I realized that we were the very group that he had most wanted to contact. We were posterity. His message was ultimately cryptic, indecipherable, open to interpretation. He had become postmodern despite his antic humor.

As we stood holding hands, Christopher, Chantal, David, and I, all of us connected and interconnected, Shakespeare's image felt part of us. He was the central setting of a finely wrought ring, the pollen-dappled calyx of a passion flower, the place where all our nerves coalesced. We remained suspended in that glow from the projector until the music ended and the image disappeared before us as suddenly as had appeared. The rest was silence, and in that silence we lingered. Our hands dropped, but I saw that Christopher's and Chantal's didn't.

17

TELL ME THOU LOV'ST ELSEWHERE

I felt Christopher slipping away. He was working on Pluto, the most distant of planets from the sun. Accurate to scale, he had to put Pluto at the end of the long hallway that leads to the maid's room in the back of the apartment. I almost never saw him. Our encounters dwindled and paled like sunlight that falls off by the square of the distance.

"How is it going?" I would ask.

"Okay."

"Pluto almost done?"

"Uh huh."

"What next?"

"Not much. Pluto's the end."

"Isn't there supposed to be something else out there?"

"Could be. No one knows."

"How can a solar system just end?" I asked.

"It just wears away."

"But do gravity and light just stop," I asked like a child.

"No, they weaken. They die."

"I hate that things die."

"It's the way of the world," he said with the weariness of an adult.

"I don't accept that blind cave of eternal night."

"Then you will be an unhappy man."

"I am one," I added melodramatically.

He looked up with his universe-soaked eyes. "I'm sorry."

The phone rang. It was Chantal. We agreed to meet at the Hungarian Pastry Shop. I stopped in my office on the way to the cafe and found a stack of papers from the sonnet course. I quickly looked through them. There was one entitled "Will Shakes his Spear, But Anne Hath a Way," by Jean Wilson, the feminist with salt-and-pepper hair. Gnostril had written his "Lemur and Le Mur: A Sociobiological Study of Apes, Limits, and Elizabethan Drama." And Linette had written "Black Calliope: The Dark Lady, Music, and the African Diaspora." The Jesuit's paper was called "Bardic Divine Rituals: The Religious Power of Reading Shakespeare's Sonnets Aloud Continuously." The rest of the students, the ones who had remained in the course after everyone else had left, had collectively decided to reject analysis and simply retyped the sonnets. Some illustrated them with water colors; others had done needlepoint, quilts, computer graphics, posters with photos cut out from magazines like *Seventeen* and *Elle*. Now that the time for grades had come, they all wanted something from me. I put the papers in an envelope and shoved them under my arm.

When I got to the pastry shop, with the looming cathedral across the street casting a dismal shadow, Chantal was already drinking a double espresso and munching on a croissant with apricot jam. The way the coffee smelled, the way her hair spiked up, the way the dank light filtered in through cigarette smoke made me want her again more than I ever had. I admired her. I missed our conversations.

"So what did you think?" she asked.

"Fabulous. What can I say?"

"Did you notice how he limped?"

"Yes."

"Now we can understand when he says in Sonnet 89:

> Say that thou didst forsake me for some fault,
> And I will comment upon that offense:
> Speak of my lameness, and I straight will halt,
> Against thy reasons making no defense."

"Ah!"

"Yes, and then of course we have to think of Richard the Third. Isn't it amazing to think that Shakespeare took his own physical disability and gave it to the villain."

"Amazing!" I had to say.

"So that's why he is so hung up on the perfection of this young man. He needs the complement to his own disability physically. He's old. He limps. He thinks he's unattractive."

"Well, that does happen."

She smiled. "Are you fishing for compliments?"

"One does age."

"You know I find you attractive. Experience should tell you that."

"Experience is a confusing mentor. So why not come back with . . . "

I can't. I don't *do* going back." She paused. "Did I tell you that I'm getting all kinds of incredible offers for my patent on Hündt's process?"

I thought of Norman and smiled.

"Not just from Norman, either," she countered. "I mean really big offers."

"Great."

"These are both academic offers and corporate."

"Corporate! I thought you were Fidel to my Che."

"Money doesn't belong to anyone. It's just pure use value. Better that I'm owning the means of production. Don't you think I'll put it to good use?"

"No doubt," I said. "You look great."

"Will." She looked at me for a while as if she were formulating a thought. I felt awkward and glanced around. My eye settled on her briefcase. From the tip of it protruded a hand-bound book. I looked harder. It was the one I had given Christopher. I could even see some of the flour glue, now flaking and crusty.

I didn't know what to say. My lips just silently formed his name. She followed my eyes.

"Yes. He gave it to me."

"To take is not to give," I said to myself.

"Will, you need to know something."

"I really don't want to know anything."

"But . . . "

"No, that's fine. I accept whatever there is . . . "

"But you don't . . ."

"I understand," I said magnanimously.

"You don't. You just think you do." She slammed her hand down on the table. The espressos trembled.

I returned to the apartment. There was a phone message from Norman telling me to look at today's *New York Times*. I picked up the copy Christopher had been reading and saw the headline: "Upswing in Sexual Harassment at the University." As Norman had implied, I was one of the people up doing the swinging. Not only was I mentioned, along with the accusations in Chantal's letter, but there were photos of me and Chantal, as well as me and Christopher. I tried to remember where we were when these were taken. I wondered how the *Times* could have gotten personal pictures. I suddenly recalled the photos that Chantal had shown during the Hündt display. Who had taken those? I needed to lie down and collapsed on the couch. The sun streamed in, promising the humid breath of a New York summer. I needed a vacation. I began to see people form in thin air like holograms. I saw my mother, my father, Anne, the kids—they all materialized and stood like angry ghosts pointing toward me. In the center was Shakespeare, pointing to me as well. I moaned and woke.

I decided I needed to take a walk. I wanted to think things over. As I walked out of my apartment building, I was blinded by flashes of light. Television cameras and newspaper reporters were yelling questions at me.

"Did you have sex with your students?"

"Is he up there now?"

"Are you in love?"

Someone pulled me aside and asked me if I'd be willing to be on an Oprah show about overcoming premature ejaculation. It was several blocks before I could shake the reporters from my side. When I got to my office, more were there. They had been interviewing everyone in sight. I saw one holding a microphone to Jennifer's face, and another was trying to get Gnostril to discuss the possibility that I had committed sodomy with primates. Samuel Morse, red-faced and fuming, gestured for me to enter his inner sanctum.

"Will, this is impossible. You'll have to take a leave. I suggest it begin today."

"But, I . . . aren't I innocent until proven guilty."

"Technically, yes. But you are proven guilty by this fiasco. The publicity is horrendous. The president of the university just called to say that a major donor who endowed Norman's chair will withdraw her money if you are not dealt with."

"So, as far as you are concerned, I'm to be jettisoned. And what is my crime?"

"Sexual harassment, conduct unbecoming . . . you name it."

"Love is my sin."

"Make that the heresy of self-love, Will. You got yourself into this."

"I assume you'll stand behind me. Academic freedom, and all that, Sam."

"Will, personally, I'm behind you one hundred percent. But in my role as chair of the thirteenth-best English department in the country, I have a larger responsibility. We all stand behind you as a friend and a colleague, but as an institutional body, I'm afraid we'll have to side with the administration on this. I do regret that, and I wish you all the best on a personal level."

He shook my hand and then had to take a phone call. I heard him reassuring someone about the stability of the department as I wandered out into the hallway where the reporters shoved microphones into my face and asked questions that implied my guilt. Down at the other end of the corridor, Norman was gesticulating grandiosely while being interviewed by CBS. The whole department was abuzz with the folly of fame as it flowed out of and into the television cameras.

I thought it might make sense to leave New York City for a while. I returned to my apartment, entered through the service entrance, and dodged the *paparazzi*. When I opened the door, I had a horrible sense of imminent doom. I heard sounds at the end of the long corridor. I walked down slowly, my vision jittering like a hand-held camera in a *cinema verité* film. The sounds became more distinct. I wanted to stop, but I was pulled along by the gravitational pull of the planets. I passed Jupiter, Saturn, Uranus, and at Pluto I was outside Christoper's bedroom door. I hesitated then opened it.

Because of my angle, I could not see clearly. Chantal and Christopher were naked. Christopher appeared to be tied up in a leather harness and was hanging upside down from the ceiling like a suspended planet, a new one no one had discovered that floated outside the solar system like a wandering eremite. Chantal was standing so that her face was near his penis, and his head between her legs. Her arms were around him, and she had some strange piece of plastic in her hands. They looked both beautiful in their strong polished bodies, yet horribly perverse, caught in some moment of personal obsession and humiliation. I thought I saw blood dripping down her legs and blood on his wrists. He seemed like the hanged man of the Tarot or the inverted crucifixion of St. Peter. Was theirs a bizarre communion or a baptism of bodily fluids?

Neither of them saw me. I closed the door. I left the apartment through the delivery entrance, walked the city until midnight, and returned. Christopher was now alone. He saw me and unsuspectingly said, "Will, guess what? One of my friends who produces performance pieces came over to here, and he loved the solar system. He thinks I could do a great performance piece around it. He's going to set something up at La Mama."

"Chris, I saw Chantal today." I was going to say that I saw them, but stopped. "I met her in the coffee shop."

"Her?"

"Chantal."

"Yes."

"Why does she have the book I gave you?"

"Because I gave it to her."

"And why did you do that?"

"Because I knew she was a lot more likely to write in it than I was." He wanted to end the conversation. I didn't.

"But I gave it to you."

"Yes, you did. But if you gave it to me you might as well be giving it to her."

"What does that mean? Are you . . . " I was going to say "lovers," but he said something before me.

" . . . married."

"Because you're true minds?"

"No, because we are husband and wife."

"Really! And when did you sneak off and do this?"

"About ten . . . "

"Ten . . . " I expected him to say "ten days" or "ten minutes."

" . . . years ago."

"What about . . . " I was going to say "us" but I said, " . . . your girlfriend? What was her name . . . Sarah . . . "

"Sarah Moskowitz.

"Yes, what about her?"

"She's my wife."

"Two wives?"

"Just one. Chantal is Sarah. Her real name is Sarah Shandel Moskowitz but she always hated that name. She wanted to re-make herself, so she gave herself the name Chantal Sarah Terpsikore Mukarjee."

"So she's not multicultural . . ." I found myself clinging to some thread of the story like a child with a shard of its over-caressed blanket.

"Well, she's basically Jewish with some other stuff thrown in."

"But, then, when you came here. When I met her . . . "

"Yes, it was more than just coincidence."

"You planned all this?"

"Well, not all. Not at first, but when your wife left you, we realized you needed . . . something. Your life was stuck, really, so we wanted to help, give you some . . . passion, some meaning."

"So you both fucked me? You gave me sex as alms? What are you—the Sisters of Mercy?"

"It wasn't . . . wasn't it worth it?"

I couldn't answer all at once.

"She wanted you to have something special from us."

"Like the executed man's last meal."

"Yes, like that."

"So I was given my last supper."

"You could say so."

"Well, it *was* gourmet," I said bitterly.

There was a long awkward silence punctuated by Christopher drumming his nails on the planet Venus.

"But what about love?"

"Yes, what?"

"Did you fake loving me? Did she?"

"Well, in that classic, bourgeois sense, we don't believe in love. We're actually writing a manifesto against it." I felt as if I were back months ago when Christopher first came to dinner. The conversation had come full circle.

"Remember when you first came here and we talked of getting married. You said it was a bourgeois institution. But you were married all along."

"Yes."

"Well, why did both of you get married if you didn't believe in it?"

"We got drunk one night in Vegas and we just . . . "

"Doesn't sound very principled," I said.

"Depends."

"Yes, it would. But you must think I'm a fool."

"Oh no, we would never."

"But you made me a fool."

"That wasn't our intent . . ."

I thought he should be as wise as he was cruel and not press my tongue-tied patience with too much disdain. I didn't want him to tell me anymore. I didn't want sorrow to give words to my pain. He had honesty, of a sort, but he needed wit not to tell me all. I was like a dying man who wanted only good news from the doctor. The world had grown so bad, mad slanders believed by mad ears, that I just wanted him to stare into my eyes and lie to me if necessary, tell me something other than his proud heart felt.

"So that's it?" I asked.

"That's it."

"The end?"

"If you want it to be."

I thought of my options. I could continue this ménage, perhaps I could even join in on it. But did I really want to be a satellite to their complex double-star? Did I need all the blood between them—bad or not? I could throw Christopher out. It was time. But I had the stomach for none of the above.

I need a vacation, I thought. A very long one.

When Christopher went to sleep, I packed my bags, took one last look at the Hudson, steeped in summer's nightly haze, ebbing from the dark, inner gut of the continent, and left the apartment.

18

The little Love-God lying once asleep

Mezzogiorno in the Piazza Signoria. The Mediterranean light crashed into my rumpled linen jacket like a frenzied pickpocket. I was lost in the polyglot crowd of tourists who wandered dazed and stunned, blindfolded and turned about in circles by the exigencies of travel. My first thought of escape was Italy, and my second was Florence. I had been here when I was a student backpacking through Europe. That seemed to me to have been a time of promise and possibility. I wanted to return to that moment when all was full of ripeness and ripe with fullness. I sat now in a cafe called *Rivoire*, drinking a paralyzingly cold Orvieto white, rehearsing my fate, and reading the *Herald Tribune*. I thought of the Venetian word for white wine–*ombra*. Why was white wine a shadow? Did one drink it protected from the sun under a loggia? Or when the shadows were longer at the end of the day?

It was two months since I had left New York. I had almost managed to leave the city without seeing Chantal. I wanted to, but she called me at Norman's apartment where I was staying while I got my airline tickets. I should have refused cleanly, but instead I agreed to meet her. I thought about killing her. She wanted to die after all. It would have been fitting for me to strangle her with my belt. That was how all this started. And so I'd be the condemned man. But then who would cook my last supper?

We drove up together to Arthur Avenue in the Bronx. Chantal wanted to buy some food for the next execution, which she was doing with an Italian theme since the murderer was a mafia hit man. She needed a ride. We rode up in virtual silence. I could not speak and neither could she.

We got out of the car in front of a fish market. Chantal was standing before a case of soft-shelled crabs, whose helpless flailing claws tried to snap at the unseen menace around them.

"Do you hate me?"

"Yes."

"I'm sorry."

"Sorry! You deliberately misled me. You made a fool of me. You manipulated my life like it was one of your computer images. I have no wife. I have no job. And I don't even have you."

We walked along 187th Street and entered a store with no sign over it. Chickens, pigeons, ducks were crammed into foul smelling cages. Feathers quivered on the floor.

"They're better fresh-killed," she explained to me.

A man of enormous unimportance listened to Chantal's request, took the terror-eyed chicken from the cage, held it upside down while he tied the feet together, suspended it from a scale, and weighed it. This was the last judgment for the chicken, and she knew it. She screamed, flapped, squawked, and writhed.

"Will, I know you'll never believe me, but we were doing this for you."

"For me? Oh thank you," I said watching the chicken struggling in some simple, focused, but hugely ineffective effort to keep the light in its eyes from dimming forever.

The man gave the chicken's neck a solid twist. I heard the torque of the dull crack, and the feathers slumped into the relieved gravity of things recently dead.

"We thought that if you . . . "

"Don't give yourself any solace thinking you were doing something for me. You were helping yourself to some . . ."

"But . . . " She stopped to pay for the heavy bag filled with what had been a squawking protest moments earlier. We pretended we did not know what was in it or how it got there. As we were leaving the store, I bumped against the bag and felt the solid, immobile weight. Dead chicken.

On the street, she said, "Let me tell you something, Will."

"What can you tell me?"

"When I was a child, my father used to play a game with me . . . "

"Spare me . . ."

"No, wait. He used to take me into the attic and undress me. He said he was taking photographs of me for his art, so he could draw little putti, cherubs, whatever later. He would fit me up with pretty, frilly lace things, kept touching me, adjusting things . . ."

"I'm not interested . . ."

"Listen, he would . . . "

"No. Just stop. You don't mean to tell me you were abused by your father, so you think that whatever you do to me is justified."

"Not justified, but a kind of a repetition . . . "

"Kind of a revenge, if you ask me."

"Doesn't that mean anything to you?"

"No, it doesn't. Do you think that telling me that story makes this all logical? That narrative mitigates things? So you have a story and an explanation. It doesn't change anything. I'm not your therapist, Chantal. I'm your victim."

We stepped into a bakery. The smell of bread seethed against us, making the tale she told seem momentarily part of the domestic, the hearth.

"Don't tell me any more stories," I whispered. Girls with teased hair and accents more redolent than the yeast in the air thumped bread on the marble counter, wrapped it in paper and string, and then began the process again like dancers caught in an endless choreography.

"Isn't there anything I can do for you? I'm really sorry."

She seemed as if she was going to cry. I suddenly realized this was the first time I'd ever seen her near tears.

"Whaddya want?" said one sloe-eyed keeper of the hearth.

"Semolina bread," Chantal turned, flicking the tear onto the sawdust coating the floor.

"I want," I found myself saying, "to know if you ever loved me?" I was embarrassed as soon as I said it.

The girl behind the counter looked at us as if we were on loan from some museum.

Chantal's eyes suddenly seemed to open as if they were twin camera lenses on time exposure. I looked in but could not see more.

"Sorry, I can't say that. I don't believe in love."

"But . . ."

"But, if I did. If I did believe in love. Then I would say that I loved you."

"The conditional tense," I murmured.

The counter girl's monumental hair swayed dolorously back and forth as she shook her head in contrition for us.

"The conditional is the best we get. You want more?"

How could I ask for more, having been given less? I was no Oliver Twist, so I took the bread instead, neatly wrapped and still warm. We walked out into the street.

"I've got to get some eggplant."

"Aubergine," I thought, but said, "I'm leaving."

"Don't . . ."

I didn't answer her. It was time. I began walking. She ran after me and put something in my hand. I kept walking.

She watched me recede into the crowd of shoppers. After a block, I looked back, despite myself, and saw her—something small and sad, a rune in black written against the confusion of the market street like the simple brush stroke of a Chinese paint-ing. A verticality signifying something hauntingly vague yet enormously important.

That was the last I saw of her. We didn't even kiss goodbye. Why would we? After a while, I became aware of the thing she had given me. My fingers recognized the soft, tooled leather of the book. I opened it up. It was still blank.

When I first arrived in Florence, I was senseless with all that had happened. I slept numbed hours in my *pensione* on the Oltrarno, ate desultorily, wandered aimlessly, and felt a world-weary despair. That lasted for weeks.

At one point I found myself in Le Cascine, the shaded park along the river. The heat of the day and the pain of my malaise was damped under the umbrageous overhang like a cool touch on a feverish forehead. I sat on a bench and watched the prostitutes line up along the drive. That was when I remembered.

They were all men. In my mind something went wrong. A wire crossed in my brain between the genders. Suddenly all I wanted was these beautiful women who were men. It seemed appropriate that I could combine Chantal and Christopher in one being that I could buy, use, and dispose of as I myself had been cast off. I didn't care what it was I had to do to them or they to me.

But I was cowardly, unable to act, to utter my unspeakable desire. So I sat, like a valetudinarian on a midday outing, watching the cars pull up and the young beauties climb in and drive off. Each was whisked away from me, as my hesitation became a permanent inability to express or do anything.

One day, after many hours of impotent gazing, I became aware of a prostitute approaching me. I could just make the gestalt of a slinky, female figure.

"*Che vuole?*" she said. What did I want? Did I even know?

"*Non saprei dire.*" I wouldn't know to say.

She smiled at me, at my rather formal and conditional response. There was a darkness about his look that was familiar. She was my height and the body suggested both male and female in some pleasing combination.

"*Amore,*" she said plainly, and I could see the white glint of his teeth. My pronouns were reeling in confusion. She took my hand, and we walked a bit to a darker place.

She kissed me, and I could smell her perfume, taste the red of her lipstick, the dense, rich attar of his hair. Her body felt male, but softer, female. She had breasts that were real, somehow. I truly didn't know anything. She put my hands up the meshed nylon of her thighs to between her legs, where I felt her erection. She was bigger than me, I thought. There was confusion, groping, panting, walking, and then, somehow, we were in a room in a hotel. Time disappeared into a haze of liquor, drugs, and sex. I seemed to have been there for days. When I left, I was exhausted as if my life had dripped down my legs like wax at the base of a candle.

Some days later, I went back to the park. I looked for her, but I never found him again. I tried others, but the excitement of the gender fugue was gone. My life went on in disorder like this for two months.

I looked around the piazza at the struggling hordes. I tried to find someone whom I could snare with my erotic lasso. A small Japanese woman in black flicked her hair and eyes back at me. I couldn't bring myself to look back. By now my wine had warmed, tasting nauseatingly off. I tried to remember all the news from the States. I had heard from Christopher that Chantal had cut a deal with Bill Gates at Microsoft for the Hündt project, which would now be made into a CD-ROM called "Shakespeare's Ghost," an interactive game in which PC owners could commune with the Bard. A virtual-reality version of the game would be marketed throughout the country at shopping malls so that weary consumers could take the pause that refreshes with Will Shakespeare, who would advise them on their personal problems and consumer dilemmas with apt quotes from his works. Chantal herself had managed to finish her thesis and get a job at Columbia at the same time. She would enter as an associate professor, thanks to Norman's intervention, and would teach cyber-textuality in exchange no doubt for immortalizing Norman's beefy body. Delilah, by the way, had become a full professor, so that Norman had virtually cornered the English department with his protegees.

My own fate was less appetizing. I was asked to resign and give up my tenure. In exchange for that concession, I would be able to work as a functionary in the alumni office. My salary would be figured according to some humbling algorithmic reduction that I could only barely understand. I would be able to keep an apartment, since I was still a Columbia employee, but unfortunately it would not be my current one. I would have to agree to move to a studio, and I understood that my own apartment, along with the one next door, would be combined for Chantal to make a mega-flat the likes of which had never been seen.

Christopher's orrery had become a huge success in the performance art scene. He was regarded as some kind of demented Da Vinci combined with Richard Forman, and articles had begun to appear in *The Village Voice* and *Salon.com* about this latter day Galileo *cum* Meredith Monk. He was now at work on another piece based on a scale model of the Milky Way using Hershey's Kisses as stars. That one would take at least until 2007 to complete, although the fact that the Hershey corporation was underwriting the project to the tune of a cool $350,000 gave him a handsome salary for the foreseeable future. Not a bad job for an obsessive compulsive who was also clearly a chocoholic.

Norman did in fact win the Nobel Prize for Literature. I looked at his bloated face in the *Herald Tribune* flanked by dignitaries including, to my surprise, a smiling, applauding Hillary Clinton. Whether she was there officially or simply to stand by her man was unclear. The Nobel Committee described his work as "a fragmentary succession of acerbic primitivisms reminiscent both of Whitman and Maori tribal songs that combined in one magisterial work the *zeitgeist* of European philosophy with the intuitive sagacity of folklore and religion." So, there was Norman in full regalia on the front page of the *Tribune* next to an article on the falling dollar and one on the rising tide of AIDS in Europe. I had received by mail at my *pensione* a copy of *Trysts Tropiques* signed by Norman with the dedication scrawled "To Will, without whom I would have never achieved immortality. Humble thanks."

Anne had refused to answer my letters and simply referred me to her lawyer. Divorce proceedings were going apace. If I was lucky, my children would be allowed to visit with me twice a year.

I sipped my by-now tepid wine before I remembered how bad it tasted and wiped the sweat from my brow. I was feeling particularly unwell, faint and nauseated. Perhaps I was experiencing the Stendhal syndrome? This was a strange affliction unique to Florence in which tourists begin to feel vertiginous, perhaps from overexposure to art, the heat, or simply the rapid pulse of Italian life. I paid the waiter and stumbled out into the blinding sun. The sidewalk began to career, and I had to hold onto the rusticated stone of a *palazzo* wall.

The meridional sun at its apex reminded me that I was not an Englishman, and so I walked uncertainly into the tomb-dank courtyard of the Palazzo Vecchio. There I found a marble bench, sat down, and regarded the fountain in the center of the courtyard. A bronze, contraposto cupid by Verrocchio squeezed a puny dolphin in his hands. So this was the little love god. I understood why the Greeks made him a mischievous, nasty little boy with an arrow. I looked at his pudgy cheeks and fat thighs. I could almost see fangs peeking from his full lips. The dolphin spit brackish water out of its mouth as the cupid laughed a metallic cadenza of eternal amusement.

I was a sick man, at least sadly distempered. I thought I should go for an AIDS test, but instead I decided it would be better to take the train to the mountains outside of Florence, to the spa at Montecatini where I could take the waters. Coincidentally, myth had it that those hot springs had heated up because of Cupid. When he lay sleeping, a nymph follower of the chaste Diana stole Cupid's arrow and plunged it into the source hoping the water's coolness would quench the arrow's chaotic fire of passion. But the water, instead of cooling the arrow, was brought to a boil by it. Hence the spa. A likely story, but perhaps I could find my cure in the healthful remedy of those heated sulphur waters which like a homeopathic medicine cures the illness with the poison that caused it. But when I thought of Chantal's eyes, of Christopher's arms, I knew that passion is never really cured, that love's fire heats water, and that no coolness can ever cool love.

I sat so long in that courtyard that night began to fall. Tourists came and went, but I sat staring at the cupid, wondering what I could do, what I had done.

I resolved to write something, an account of what had happened. If I could put things into words, perhaps that would help. I remembered Norman's contempt for writing as therapy, but I put that aside, as I put so much else of Norman aside. I would call the book *The Sonnets*, a kind of inspiration from Shakespeare's love-torn life, and an homage of sorts to the monograph I had originally planned. Perhaps there was something to be gained from all this.

I took out the still-blank, leather-bound book that had passed through three lives and managed to signify nothing. I opened the first empty page and wrote next to the faded letter "V": "This story begins with a mist, a fog, a foggy day . . . " There was so much to remember. How would I ever recall it all? I put my pen down for a moment. The cupid cavorted over the spewing waters which darkness had made to seem more like flowing blood than anything else. I felt unwell. The waters were flowing out, down the sides of the cistern, down the arms of Christopher, down through my being. Things were flowing away from me. Yes, I would go to Montecatini tomorrow. I would get better there. From the top of the mountain, I would look at the prospect of Tuscany as it stretched to the Mediterranean, the ancient valley through which flowed the vein of the Arno, the olive and grape crusted hills. I would look out on these like a life looking back on itself. I would bathe in the rejuvenating waters like a dried flower coming back to life.

And then I would begin to write.